BACKSTORIES

DC COMICS
BATMAN ™
GOTHAM CITY'S GUARDIAN

By Matthew K. Manning
Illustrated by Steven Gordon
Batman created by Bob Kane

SCHOLASTIC INC.

ISBN 978-0-545-86816-7

10 9 8 7 6 5 4 3 2 16 17 18 19 20

Printed in the U.S.A. 40
First printing 2016

Book design by Rick DeMonico

Thank you to designer Michael Regan, and artists George Corsillo and Freddie E. Williams II for their additional contributions to the artwork in this book.

CONTENTS

Foreword... 5

Friends, Foes, and Family.................. 8

Chronology.. 12

Chapter One: Before Batman...................17

Chapter Two: I Shall Become a Bat........ 27

Chapter Three: The Equipment 39

Chapter Four: Learning Curve 55

Chapter Five: The Dynamic Duo........... 71

Chapter Six: Justice for All 83

Chapter Seven: The Allies....................... 91

Chapter Eight: The Enemies 97

Chapter Nine: The Future....................119

Fast Facts 122

Glossary.. 126

Index.. 128

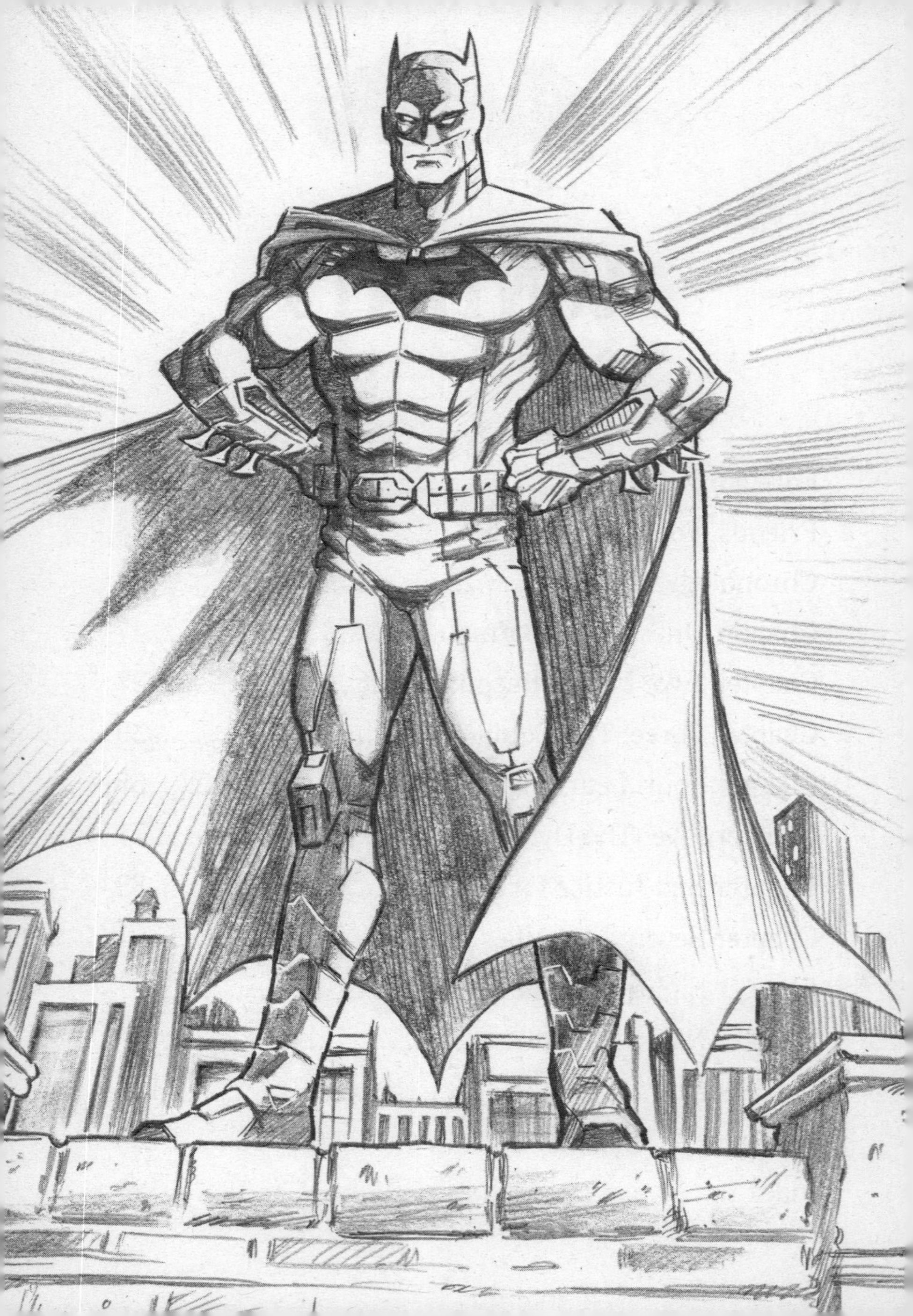

Foreword
by Batman

When I was young, I lost my parents to a random act of violence. We were walking out of a movie theater, after watching a Zorro film I'd begged them to see. My mother even wore her favorite pearls, for my sake, so it would seem like a special occasion. It would be the last time she ever wore them.

Before that night, I thought I knew fear. Just months earlier, I'd fallen into the cave system that ran beneath our mansion. A bat flew out of the shadows directly at me. I cowered, hiding my head in my arms. But it never touched me. It was like I didn't even matter. It kept on flying up and out of the cave. When my father found me, I was shaking in fear.

That night after the movies, it was like my experience in the cave all over again. Something came out of the shadows. But this time, it was a man. He pointed his gun at my parents, and there was a scuffle. Those prized pearls bounced one by one on the dirty pavement as he pulled his trigger. But he never aimed his gun at me. It was like I still didn't matter. In that moment, I became an orphan. I became another victim of Gotham City's rising crime. But if I had my way, I was going to be the last. If I had my way, I was going to finally matter.

On the day my parents were buried, I made a solemn vow. I promised to never let another innocent person suffer the same fate as my parents. I vowed to become something more than a man. I vowed to turn my darkest fears into something that would give me strength.

From that day on, my training began. I traveled the world to study with the most elusive masters of martial arts and detective work. I trained my body and mind to a level I had never thought possible. And then I returned to Gotham City and began my war on crime.

I have become much more than a scared little boy in a Gotham City alleyway. I have made myself into a frightening thing. I am the force that keeps criminals awake at night. I am the reason they look over their shoulders in fear when walking down a dimly lit street. To them, I am a creature of the shadows, Gotham City's dark protector. I am Batman.

Friends, Foes, and Family

Batman

After tragedy forever changed Bruce Wayne's world, he took on the identity of Batman. He is an expert detective and a master of many martial arts. Using high-tech gadgets and vehicles, the Dark Knight wages an endless war on crime.

Robin

Like Bruce Wayne, Dick Grayson also lost his parents at a young age. Taken in as Wayne's ward, Grayson soon became Batman's partner, Robin the Boy Wonder. He would later become a hero in his own right as the vigilante Nightwing.

Batgirl

Barbara Gordon, the daughter of Batman's ally Police Commissioner James Gordon, used her expertise in gymnastics and martial arts to follow Batman's example and become the heroic Batgirl.

The Joker

The Joker, formerly a criminal called the Red Hood, fell into a vat of chemicals during an encounter with Batman, and was forever changed from the Red Hood into the maniacal Clown Prince of Crime called the Joker.

The Penguin

Oswald Cobblepot came from one of Gotham City's oldest families. However, greed caused him to seek out a life of crime as one of the city's most notorious criminals: the Penguin.

Catwoman

Selina Kyle is the flip side to Batman's heroic persona as the thief Catwoman. While she sometimes helps the Dark Knight with his cases, she is a master thief who can't seem to stay on the right side of the law.

The Riddler

Edward Nygma embarked on a life of crime in order to match his wits with those of the Dark Knight. As the Riddler, he leaves clues to his crimes that in many cases only Batman can solve.

Alfred Pennyworth

Alfred Pennyworth, the Wayne family's butler and a highly trained soldier, helped raise Bruce Wayne after Bruce lost his parents. Still with Batman, Alfred not only takes care of Wayne Manor, but he also aids Batman on his missions from the safety of the Batcave.

Chronology

Bruce Wayne is
born to Thomas and
Martha Wayne.

As a young boy, Bruce
falls into a hole in his
yard. He lands in a
dark cave where he is
terrified by the bats
that live there.

As a young adult,
Bruce returns to
Gotham City.

A bat flies through
a window of Bruce's
study. It inspires him to
become Batman.

The Riddler begins
his criminal career.

After seeing Batman in
action, Selina Kyle dons
a costume, becomes
Catwoman, and starts
her life as a thief.

Bruce's parents are
killed by a mugger.

Bruce begins
traveling the world,
training his body and
mind.

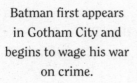

Batman first appears
in Gotham City and
begins to wage his war
on crime.

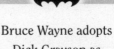

Batman confronts
the Red Hood,
causing him to fall
into chemicals and
become the Joker.

The Caped Crusader
battles the Penguin
as the villain tries
his hand at robbery
by using trick
umbrellas.

Bruce Wayne adopts
Dick Grayson as
his ward. Shortly
afterward, Robin
begins partnering
with Batman.

Batman joins other
like-minded heroes
and forms the
Justice League.

Batgirl debuts on the
Super Hero scene,
donning a costume
inspired by Batman.

The second Robin,
Jason Todd, is
murdered by the
Joker. (Jason
later returns as a
vigilante, taking the
identity of the new
Red Hood.)

Batman is joined by a
third Robin, Tim Drake,
who later calls himself
Red Robin.

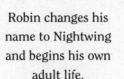

Robin changes his name to Nightwing and begins his own adult life.

Batman takes in a new ward, Jason Todd, who becomes the new Robin.

Batman meets his son, Damian Wayne, and soon adopts him as his newest Robin.

The Dark Knight continues his crusade against crime alongside his many allies.

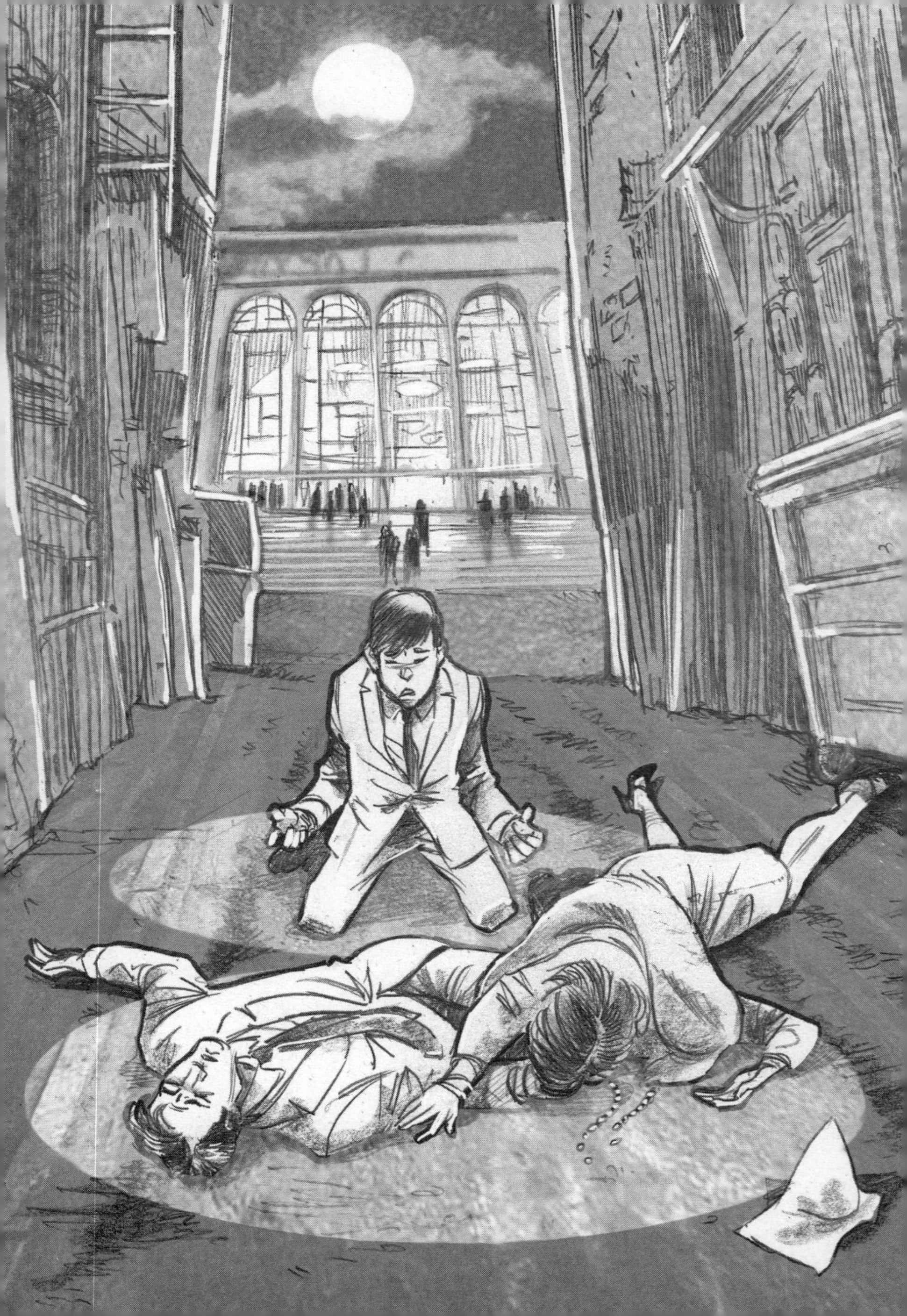

CHAPTER ONE

BEFORE BATMAN

Bruce Wayne was born to wealthy parents, Thomas and Martha Wayne. A bright and adventurous young man, Bruce idolized his mother and father. He excelled in school and did his best to live up to his family's high standards.

One afternoon, while exploring the yard outside Wayne Manor, a young Bruce fell through a hole into a large cave. He lay on the floor of the dark cavern, injured and terrified. Just then, a bat shot out of the shadows directly toward him. Bruce screamed

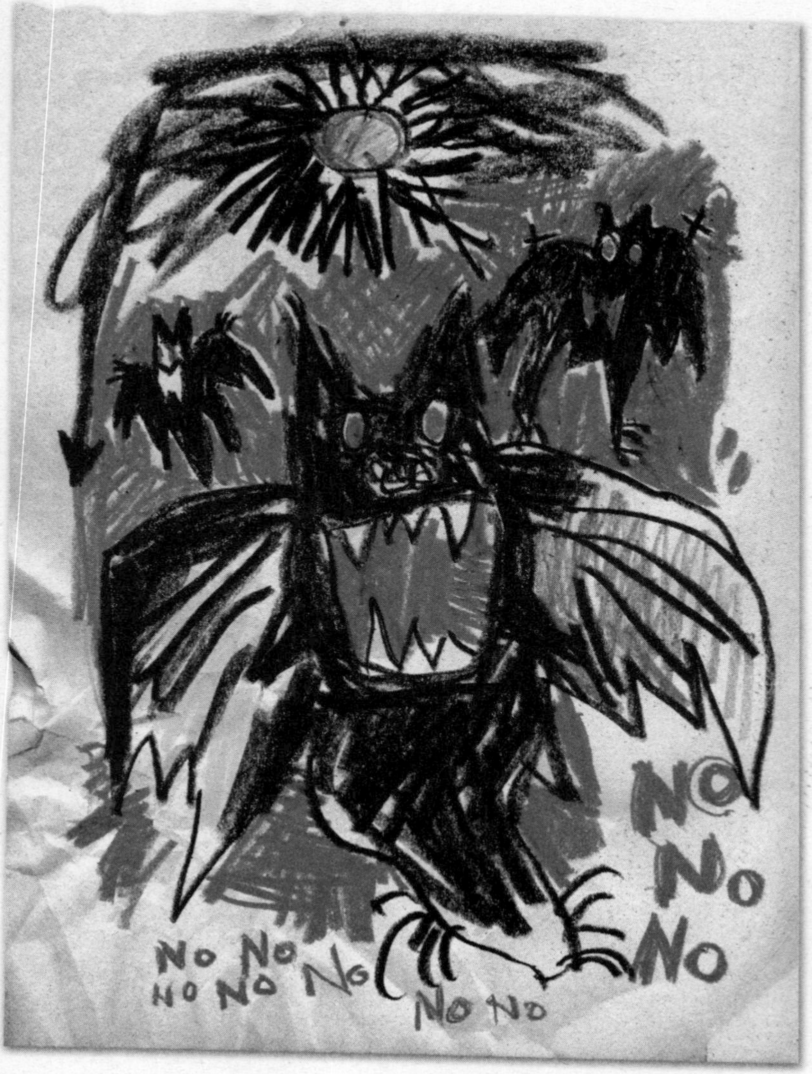
NO
No
No
No No
No No No
No No

A YOUNG BRUCE WAYNE DREW THIS IMAGE OF HIS ENCOUNTER WITH A BAT AFTER HIS FATHER PULLED HIM OUT OF THE CAVES BELOW WAYNE MANOR.

in horror until his parents heard his cries. Thomas soon found Bruce and hauled him up to safety. But the damage had been done. From that day on, young Bruce had a severe fear of bats.

Bruce loved heroics from an early age. His favorite hero was the swashbuckling character Zorro. He even dressed up like the legendary character one Halloween. When Bruce learned that *The Mark of Zorro* was playing at the Monarch Theatre in Gotham City, he begged his parents to take him. Thomas and Martha didn't want to let their son down, so

they agreed. In fact, they decided to make that night quite the event. Martha even wore her best pearls for the occasion.

After the movie was over, the Waynes walked down a dark street named Park Row. Suddenly, small-time criminal Joe Chill stepped out of the shadows. He pointed a gun at the Waynes and demanded Martha's necklace. Thomas tried his best to calm down the criminal. But there was no reasoning with Chill. He panicked, fired his gun, and shot and killed both Martha and Thomas Wayne. He retreated into the night, leaving young Bruce alive but very afraid.

That night, everything changed for Bruce. His childhood was over. He made a vow on his parents' graves to protect the innocent people of Gotham City in any way he could. He took that promise very seriously, and planned to build his life around it.

BRUCE WAYNE KEPT THE NEWSPAPER FROM THE DAY AFTER HIS PARENTS WERE KILLED. YEARS LATER, HE TRACKED DOWN THE GUNMAN TO BRING HIM TO JUSTICE.

All the News
from Gotham

Gotham City Herald

CITY EDITION

Partly to mostly cloudy. Unseasonably cool. Highs in the low 60's, low 50's in the evening. Showers likely in the morning.

50 CENTS

..., . . . XXLVII ★ ★ ★ ★ ★ ★ ★ ★ ★ ★ TUESDAY, JUNE 27, 19[illegible] ★ ★ ★ ★ ★ ★ ★ ★ ★ ★

WAYNE DOUBLE MURDER

CITY'S FIRST FAMILY SLAIN BY WOULD-BE MUGGER

By NELSON MAJORS

PARK ROW—An evening family outing gave way to a night of heartbreak and loss as renowned humanitarians and socialites Thomas and Martha Wayne were shot and killed last night after exiting the Monarch Theatre. Surviving the murder was their young son, Bruce, who also served as the crime's only witness.

According to reports, the Wayne family had attended an 8:50 screening of the 1920 Douglas Fairbanks classic "The Mark of Zorro." The couple was last seen exiting the Monarch Theatre's side doors, led by their enthusiastic son, who was apparently quite taken with the film. One witness said that the boy was acting out Mr. Fairbanks' title role, carving imaginary Z's into the air with the aid of a rolled up newspaper.

But that youthful innocence would be lost just minutes later as the family, apparently en route to rendezvous with their chauffeur and trusted family butler, Alfred Pennyworth, was gunned down by an unknown assailant in an apparent mugging gone awry.

From what police have been able to discern from Bruce Wayne, the mugger apparently emerged from the shadows, demanding Martha Wayne hand over the pearl necklace she was wearing. Thomas then stepped in front of his wife, only to be greeted by a single shot in the chest from the assailant's handgun. Martha was then shot in turn, before the murderer fled the alleyway. The coroner has confirmed the time of death for both Thomas and Martha Wayne as 10:47 p.m.

When police arrived a few minutes later, they found the young Bruce Wayne kneeling near the bodies of his two fallen parents.

"It was bad," said James Hall, one of the first officers on the scene. "The kid had this look in his eye. He was broken up, but almost calm about it. Not like shock. I've seen shock. This was something else. I've never seen it before. Hope I don't ever have to again."

Police have not released the names of any suspects at this time, but sources inside the department have stated that they do not believe this violent act was premeditated or planned in any way.

Heir to the Wayne family fortune and CEO of Wayne Enterprises, Thomas Wayne was a prominent surgeon and philanthropist, known by the public at large mainly for his work with dozens of charities, both local and as far abroad as the third-world nation of Santa Prisca. Wayne specialized in tackling difficult to near-impossible surgical operations, often astounding his peers in the medical profession with his remarkable success rate. Always one for a challenge, Wayne would more often than not work on a pro-bono basis in an apparent need to give back to the community that had been so good to his family for generations.

Thomas Wayne had met socialite and fellow charity supporter Martha Kane through mutual friends some years ago, and the two had embarked upon a romance that immediately caught the public's eye. The daughter of another of Gotham's richest families and a fixture on the Gotham City social scene, Kane had carved out a name for herself in the philanthropic world by founding a medical clinic for Gotham's destitute alongside her good friend, the well regarded family practitioner Dr. Leslie Thompkins.

With their marriage and the announcement of the birth of their son, Bruce, Thomas and Martha Wayne were quickly elevated from their status as Gotham's favorite couple to Gotham's first family.

Though like most individuals cast into the spotlight, a few detrimental rumors have surfaced about their pasts, the names Thomas and Martha Wayne have nonetheless become as synonymous with Gotham as the city's infamous architecture or its vigilante champion of the 1940's,

continued on page A3

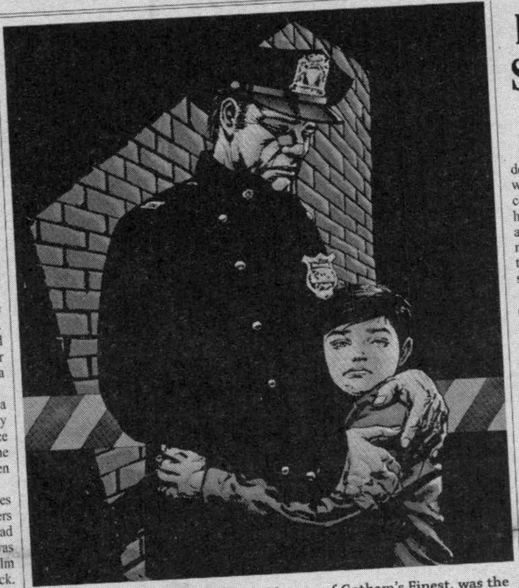

Bruce Wayne, seen here comforted by one of Gotham's Finest, was the sole survivor of the brutal double homicide.

East End Shooting?

By MIKE W. GOLDEN

EAST END—Several residents of the city's infamous warehouse district have come forward claiming to have heard gunshots near a storage facility late last night. By each account, there were at least three shots fired at a little before 11 p.m. Witnesses also claim to have later seen several police cars arrive on the scene.

Despite these seemingly independent statements, police are denying any such incident, saying no disturbance was reported last night and no police were called to that particular area. Captain Loeb was unavailable for comment, but sources inside the police department noted that it would not be unusual for a

continued on page A22

Most of U.S. Feeling Impact of Gas Crisis

Frustration Over Station Lines is Bringing on More Violence

By KEVIN REAGAN

The shortage of gasoline, which began on the West Coast and has now reached crisis proportions in much of the Northeast, is beginning to be felt in other parts of the country.

From the Gulf Coast to the Great Lakes region to the Pacific Northwest, more motorists are finding it difficult to get gasoline. Stations are shortening their daily hours and more of them are closing completely on one weekend day. Several metropolitan public transit systems have had a dramatic increase in riders in recent months.

Motorist Shot In Dallas

There has been violence. Last week two persons were shot in Gotham City, and on Sunday night in Dallas

State Argues Fate of Modern Day Bonnie and Clyde's Son

By GRANT JORGENSEN

STAR CITY—In an ongoing story that's fascinated and horrified a nation, the future of the young son of Carol and Matthew Morrison, better known to the public by the nickname the "Beatnik Butchers," is still up in the air, according to city officials.

When his parents were killed in a shootout last

Police Department. "He'd gone completely feral and was screaming at all the officers on the scene, calling us murderers."

It's this violent behavior that has instigated a fierce debate in the courtroom, as to the boy's sanity, as well as his complicity in the over four dozen murders attributed to his parents. While some have painted a picture

OPEC Factions Clash Over Oil Price

By FAROUK AWARI

GENEVA—The Organization of Petroleum Exporting Countries ended the first day of a price-fixing conference here tonight

Saudis Are Ready to Yield on Increase From $14.55 if Surcharges are Dropped

"There will be a price

est exporter and producer of 17 to 20 percent of the world's oil, which is insisting on an increase to $17 to $18 a barrel.

At the opening session of the OPEC conference this morning, Sheik Ahmed

Abdoul Aramco's oil

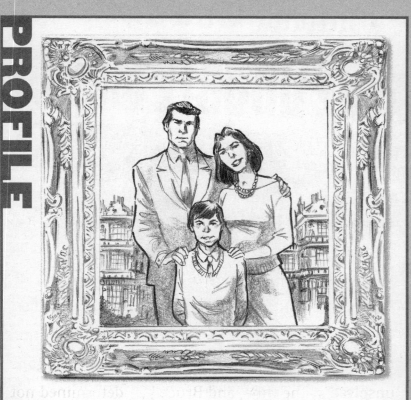

Thomas and Martha Wayne

Thomas and Martha Wayne were quite well-known throughout Gotham City. Thomas had inherited the Wayne family fortune, but nevertheless became a prominent surgeon as well as Wayne Enterprises' CEO. Martha was a renowned philanthropist, and was well recognized in even the most elite social circles. The two lived in a giant mansion called Wayne Manor with their young son, Bruce, and their loyal butler, Alfred Pennyworth. They doted on Bruce, helping him develop a strong moral character and a sense of civic responsibility.

With his parents gone, Bruce only had Alfred, the family butler, to raise him, and a kindhearted friend of the Waynes', Dr. Leslie Thompkins. As a doctor who would later run a free clinic in one of Gotham City's poorest neighborhoods, Leslie would instill in Bruce the idea of helping the unfortunate. Meanwhile, Alfred did his best to raise the boy. But having little experience with children, Alfred let Bruce run his own life, trusting his young master's judgment. Bruce began to obsess over his studies, learning everything he could about criminology and detective work. His parents' murder case had gone unsolved at the time, and Bruce was determined not to let that happen to other victims.

As a teenager, Bruce enrolled in a variety of schools including Gotham Academy and the Gotham Preparatory School for Boys, but soon began taking long sabbaticals from his studies. He never explained his absences to his friends, including roommate Harvey Dent. Eventually, Bruce would leave school altogether

PROFILE

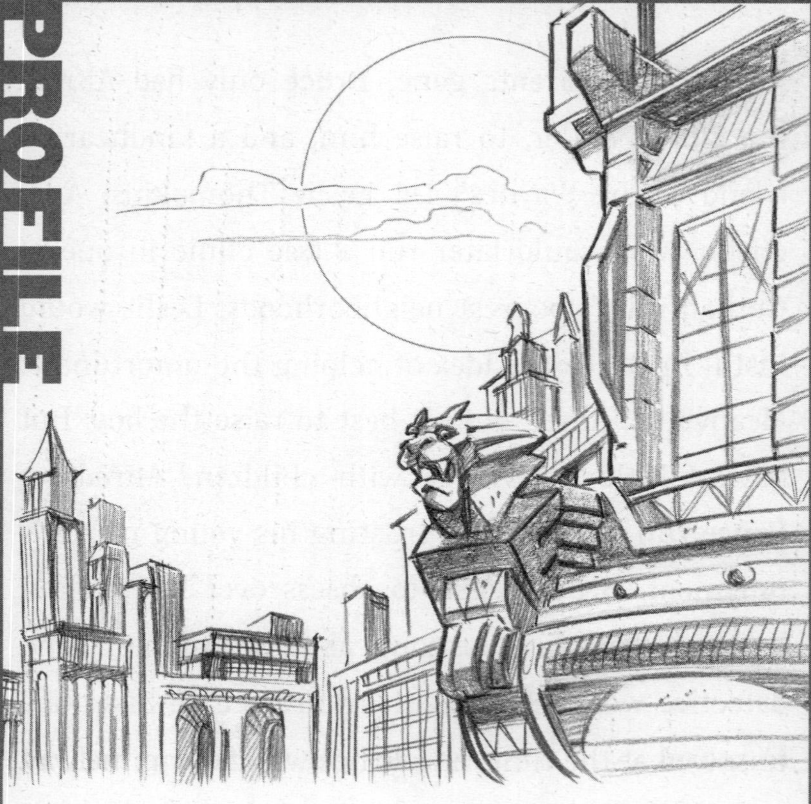

Gotham City

One of the largest cities in the country, Gotham City is strikingly unique in appearance. The buildings are a mix of art deco and Gothic architecture, and seem to be built right on top of one another. Once a hub of commerce, Gotham City fell on hard times when two of its shining stars—Thomas and Martha Wayne—were murdered. In fact, the street on which the Waynes were murdered, Park Row, became known as Crime Alley.

to begin his true studies in full.

He traveled the globe, studying with some of the most brilliant minds on the planet. From inventors to martial artists, from detectives to actors, Bruce took in everything he could to prepare. His training took years and a good deal of the Wayne family fortune. Bruce had no one to keep him company but the people he'd meet along the way. Often, he would use fake names in order to protect his Bruce Wayne identity. He knew that if he was going to operate as a crime fighter, he would need to distance his regular life from his secret life.

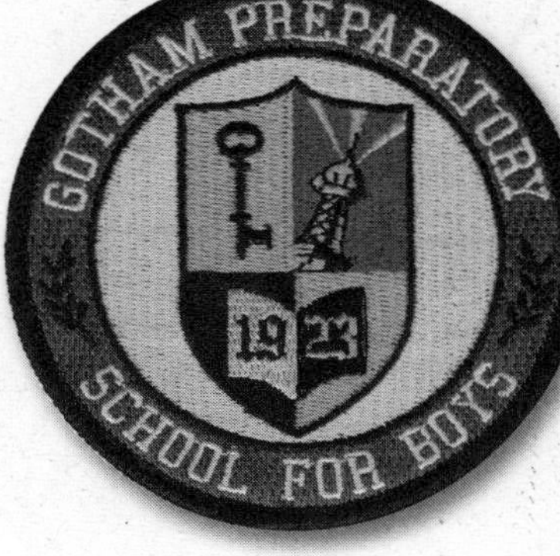
GOTHAM PREPARATORY
1923
SCHOOL FOR BOYS

DURING HIS TIME IN PREP SCHOOL, BRUCE MOSTLY KEPT TO HIMSELF. HE WAS VERY SERIOUS ABOUT HIS EDUCATION AND SHARPENING HIS ALREADY-BRILLIANT MIND.

After many years away from Gotham City, Bruce finally returned home. He had grown into a man, one with a true purpose and a mission.

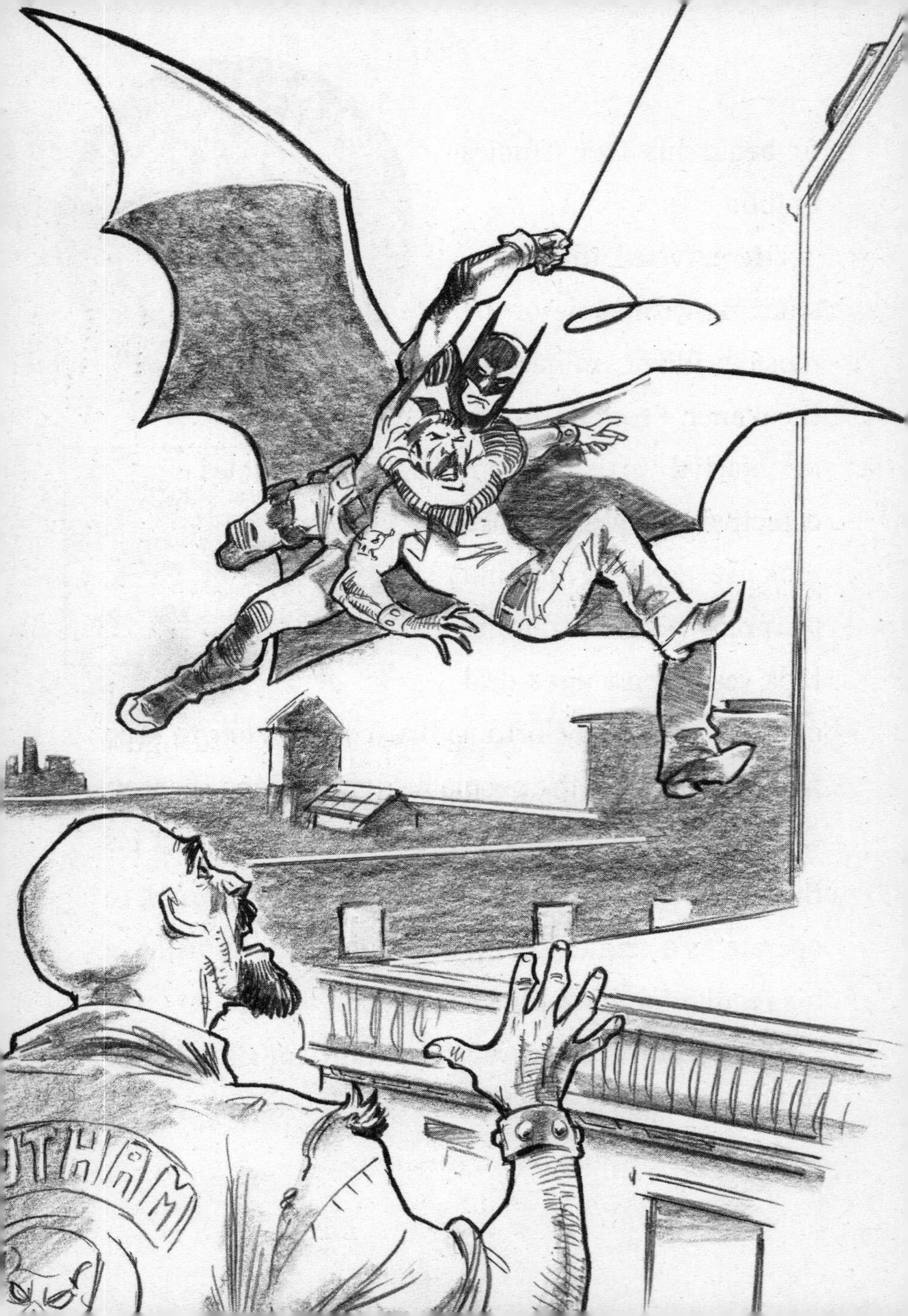
THAM

CHAPTER TWO

I SHALL BECOME A BAT

Soon after Bruce Wayne returned to Gotham City, criminals began spotting a weird figure in the shadows. Batman was a mystery to both the criminal underground and the police force alike. Some considered him merely an urban legend. Others swore he was a supernatural creature that was preying on those who dared to break the law.

This was exactly how Bruce Wayne wanted it. Bruce had realized that criminals were a superstitious and cowardly lot. He knew that he needed to strike fear into their hearts to become an effective hero and fulfill the vow he made all those years ago. After a rather unsuccessful early foray into crime fighting, Bruce took inspiration from the very animal that had so frightened him as a child.

As Bruce sat in his father's study one night, a bat flew through his window. It perched on top of the bust of Thomas Wayne. It seemed to stare at Bruce from across the room. In that moment, Bruce

remembered being young and afraid. He remembered falling into the caverns below Wayne Manor as a bat flew directly at him, and in that moment, he realized that he knew just how to instill fear in others, too.

To that end, Bruce designed the first Batman costume. It included batlike ears, a cape, and a Utility Belt to house the

PROFILE

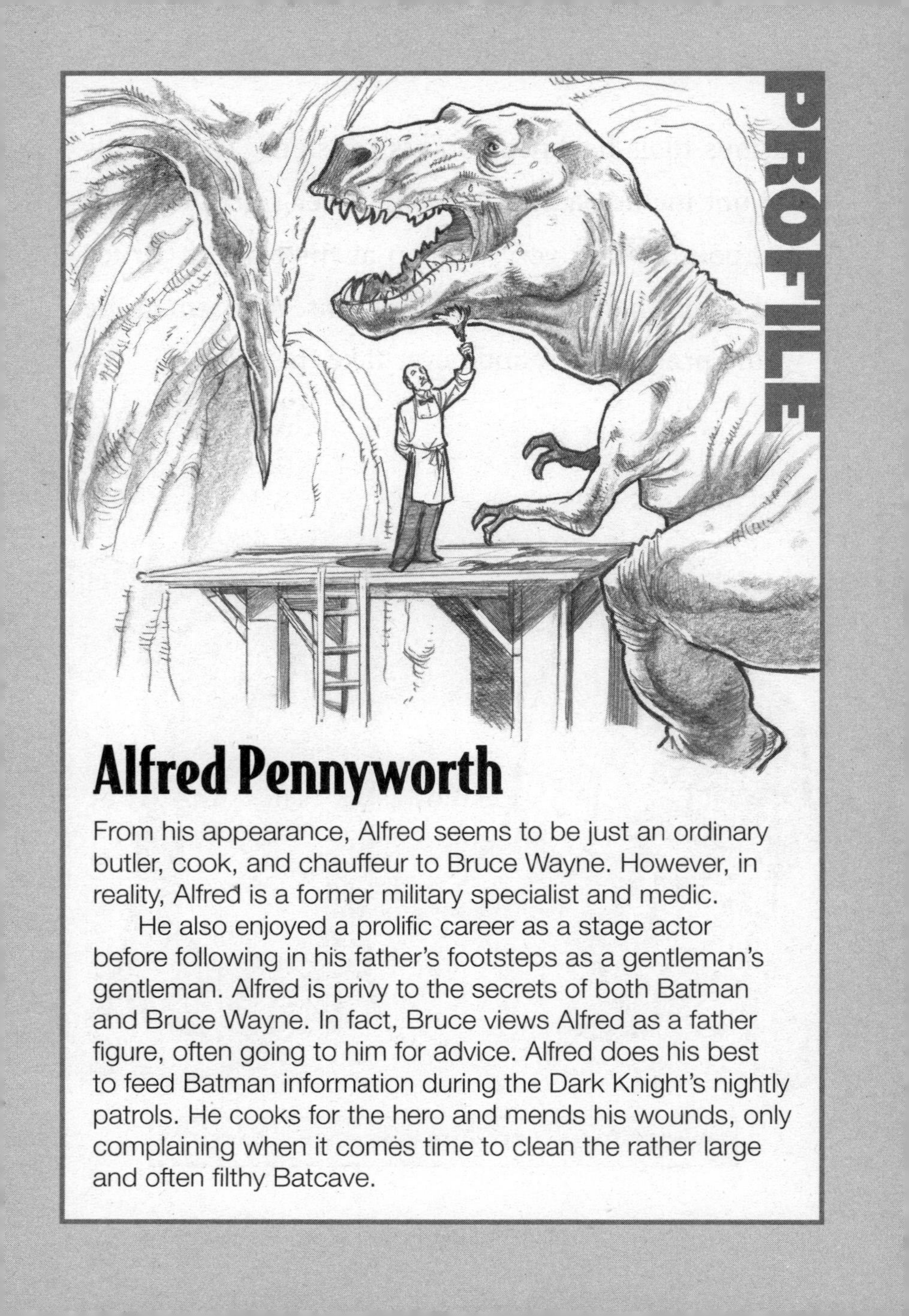

Alfred Pennyworth

From his appearance, Alfred seems to be just an ordinary butler, cook, and chauffeur to Bruce Wayne. However, in reality, Alfred is a former military specialist and medic.

He also enjoyed a prolific career as a stage actor before following in his father's footsteps as a gentleman's gentleman. Alfred is privy to the secrets of both Batman and Bruce Wayne. In fact, Bruce views Alfred as a father figure, often going to him for advice. Alfred does his best to feed Batman information during the Dark Knight's nightly patrols. He cooks for the hero and mends his wounds, only complaining when it comes time to clean the rather large and often filthy Batcave.

various tools he'd need on his missions. Those tools did not include a gun, however. Ever since Joe Chill had pointed that very weapon at his parents, Bruce had a true hatred of lethal firearms. As Batman, he would protect lives, and never take them.

BRUCE'S EARLY ATTEMPTS TO DESIGN A BATSUIT.

PROFILE

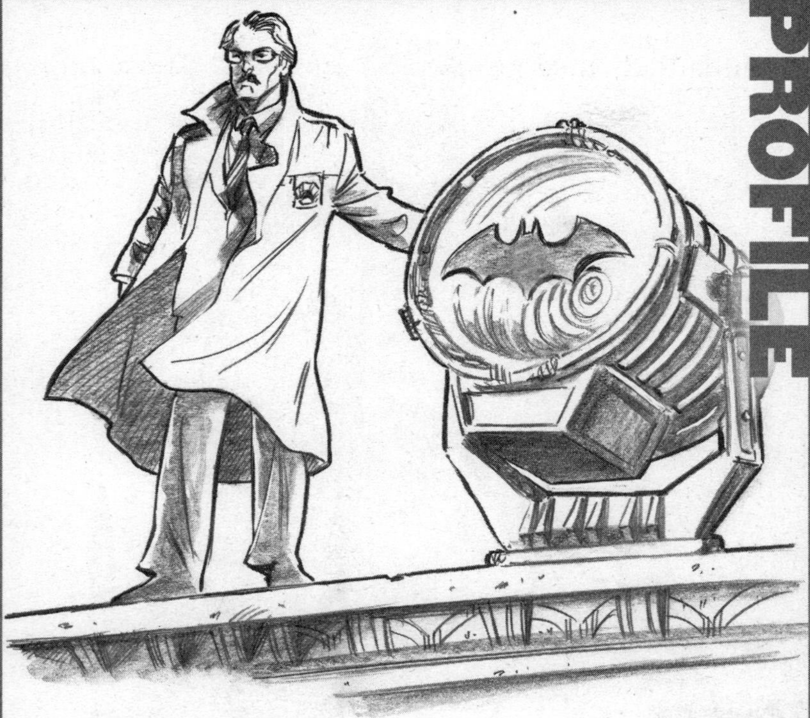

Commissioner Gordon and the Gotham City Police Department

When Batman first began his career in Gotham City, the police were nearly as corrupt as the criminals. However, a young detective named James Gordon sought to change all of that. An honorable and effective cop, Gordon worked his way up the ladder to commissioner. He even formed a rather unorthodox partnership with Batman along the way. When he needs Batman's help, Commissioner Gordon summons the Dark Knight by shining the famous Bat-Signal in the Gotham City sky.

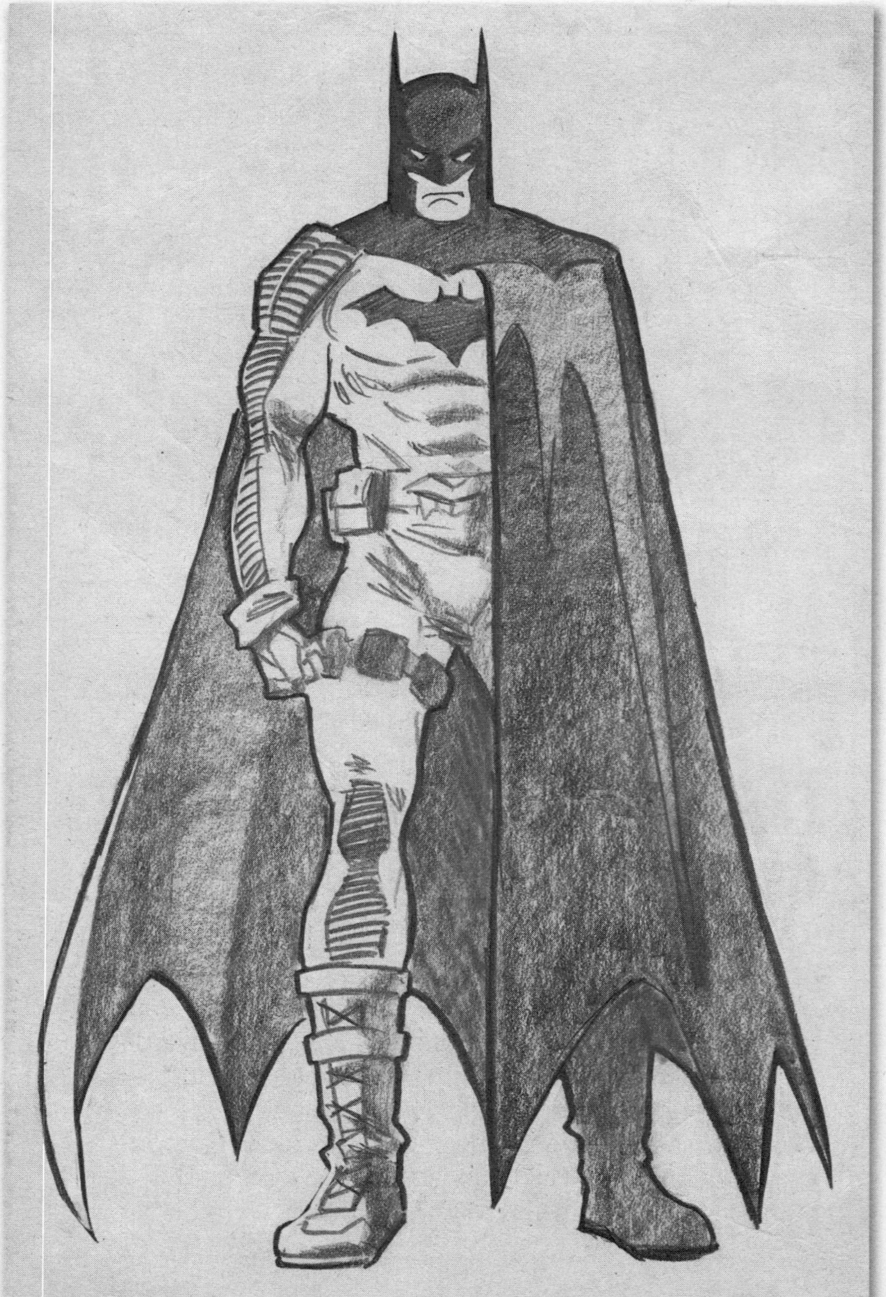

WHILE HE DOESN'T HAVE A BACKGROUND IN ART, BRUCE WAYNE HAND-SKETCHED SEVERAL DIFFERENT CONCEPTS FOR HIS BATSUIT BEFORE ALFRED CREATED THE ORIGINAL PROTOTYPE.

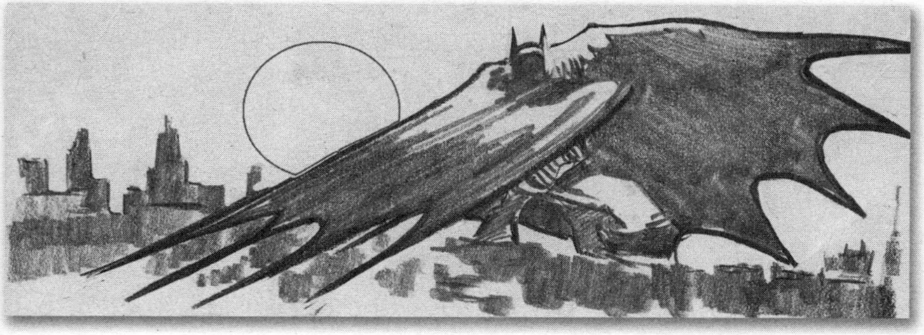

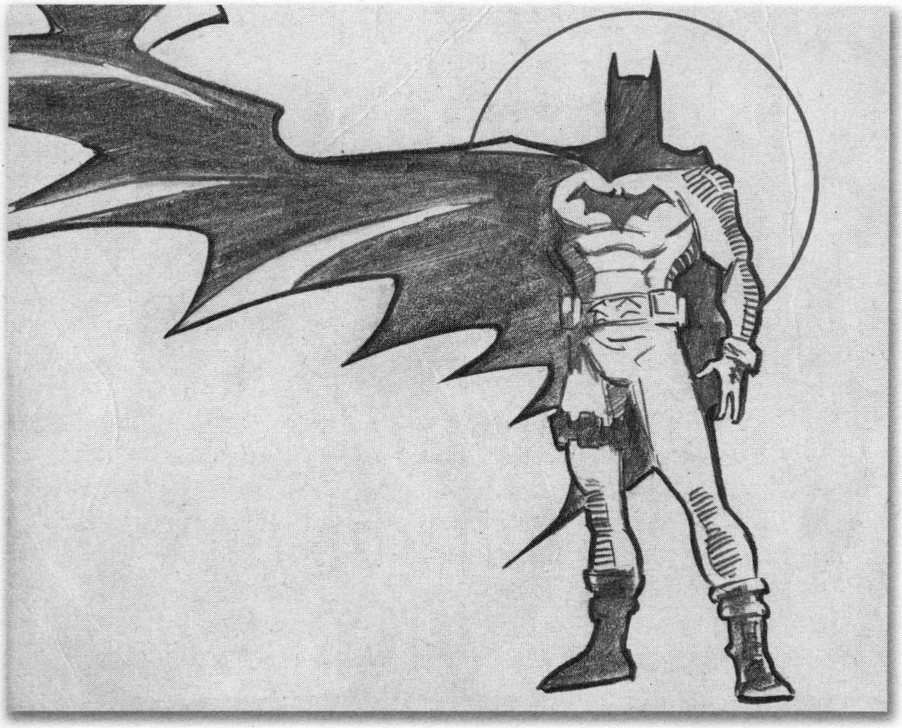

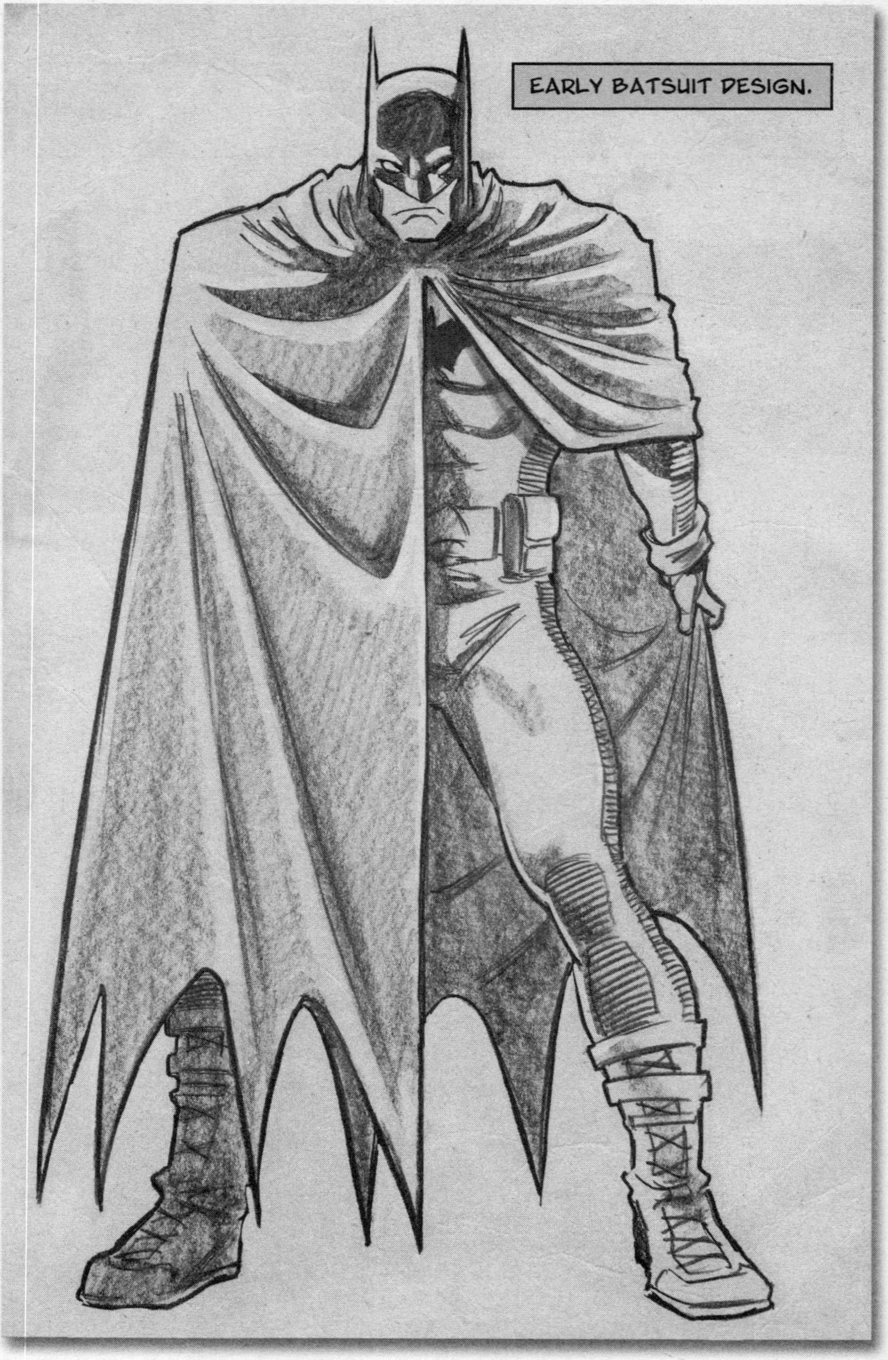
EARLY BATSUIT DESIGN.

During the day, Bruce Wayne set out to continue his father's work at Wayne Enterprises. He remained a figurehead for the company, even when later, to better concentrate on his mission as Batman, he handed off most of the day-to-day work to an old and trusted friend, Lucius Fox. Lucius was a savvy businessman and inventor, whose technological innovations have been used time and time again to further Batman's career.

LUCIUS FOX WAS ONE OF THOMAS WAYNE'S MOST TRUSTED EMPLOYEES, AND AN EXTREMELY INTELLIGENT MAN. WHEN BRUCE TOOK OVER HIS FATHER'S BUSINESS, HE WOULD PLACE THE SAME FAITH IN LUCIUS.

While Bruce contributed to many noble causes through his charitable Wayne Foundation, he appeared to be a socialite who wanted nothing more than to party his life away. In order to distance himself from Batman, he willingly led the public to believe that he was nothing more than a member of the idle rich.

However, when the moon was high, Bruce used his keen wit, brilliant mind, and his new Batsuit during his nightly patrols as Batman. His suit was even more effective than he had ever dreamed. Criminals were terrified of him, and even the police seemed to fear him. He had become the Dark Knight, and Gotham City would never be the same.

BRUCE WAYNE SOCIALIZING AT A FUND-RAISER AT WAYNE MANOR.

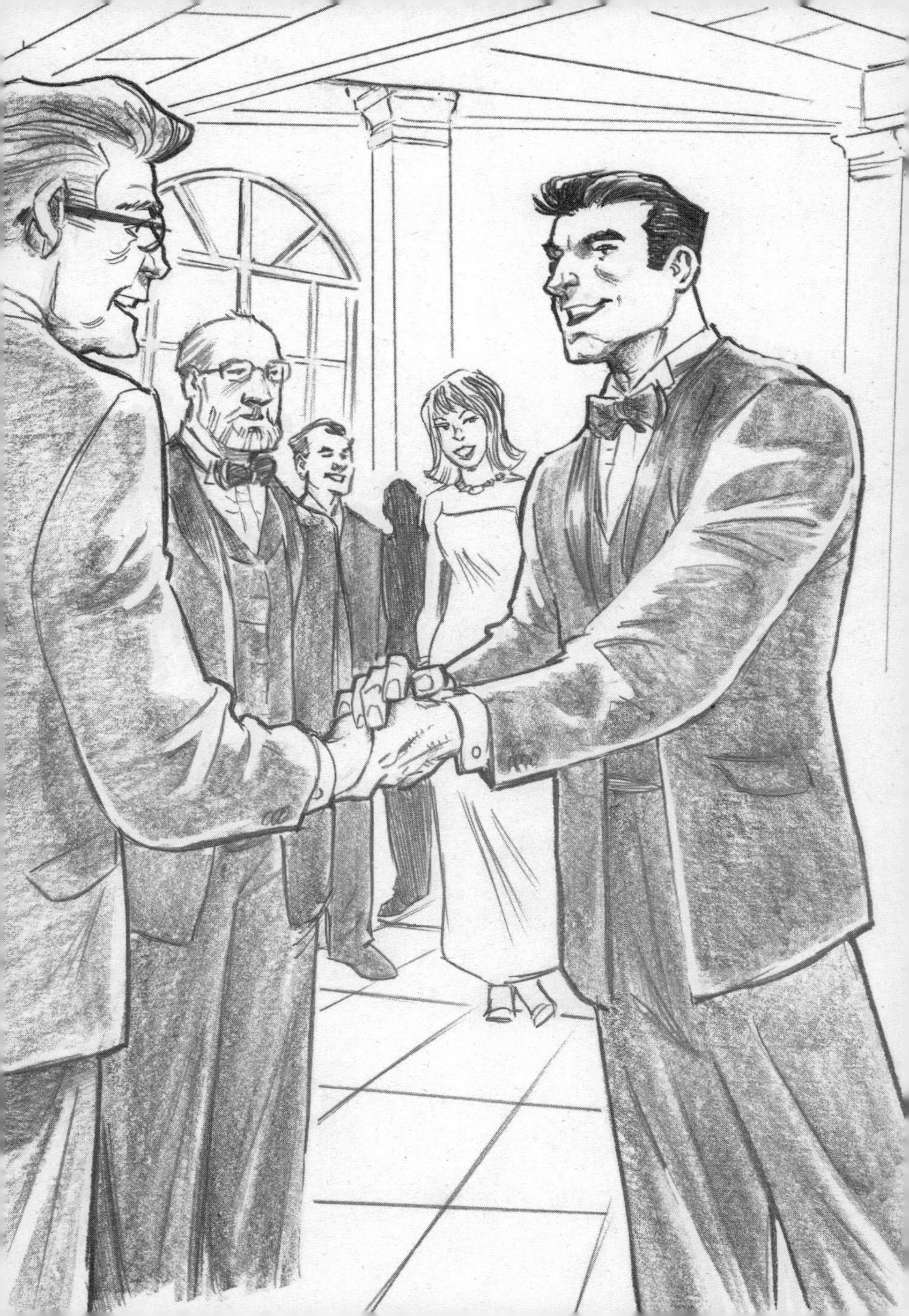

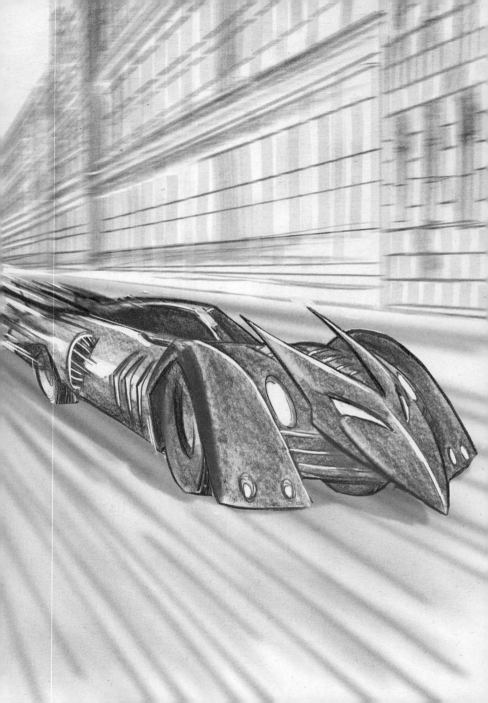

CHAPTER THREE

THE EQUIPMENT

Unlike most other Super Heroes, Batman doesn't have the extra help of superpowers. He is forced to take on the criminal element with only his wits and skills. To give him an advantage, the Caped Crusader employs an arsenal of gadgets and vehicles. These range from a handheld Batarang to the awe-inspiring Batmobile.

When he first began his career, Batman kept things rather simple. He moved from rooftop to rooftop with the help of tools like grappling hooks.

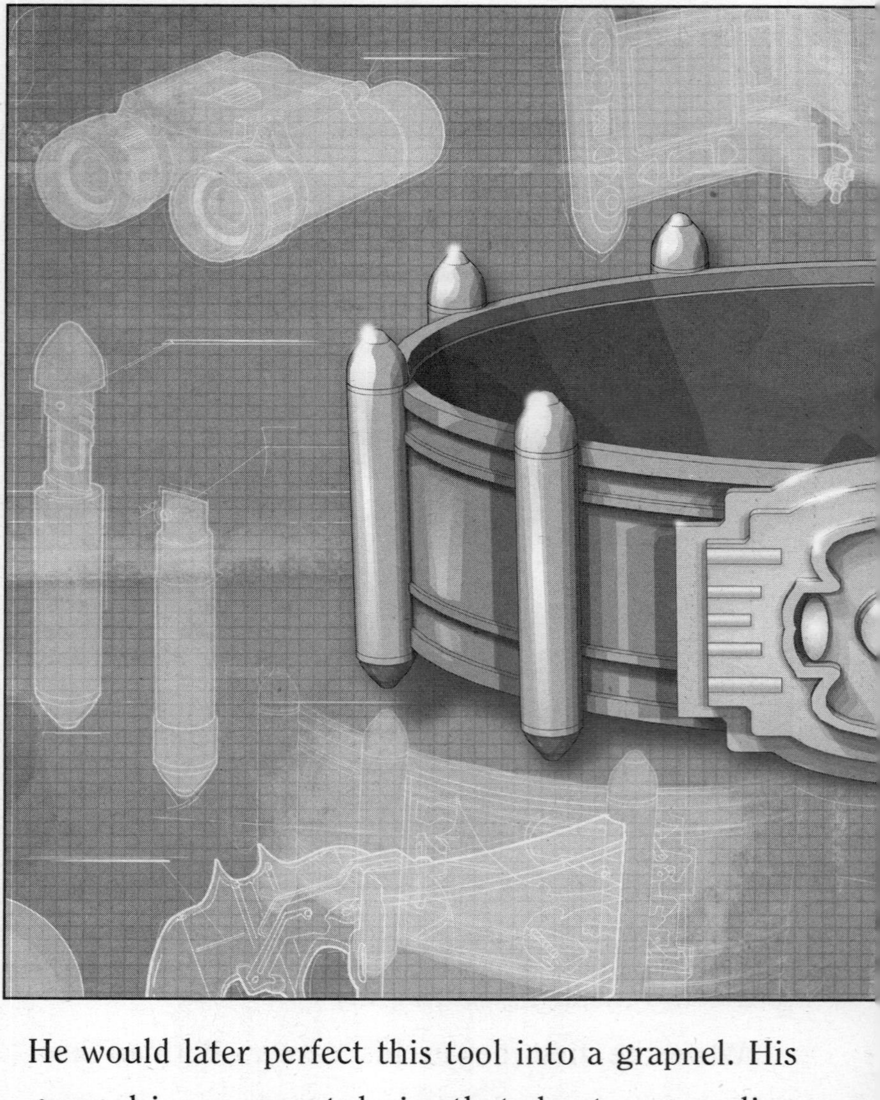

He would later perfect this tool into a grapnel. His grapnel is a compact device that shoots a grappling hook and recoils its line with the push of a button.

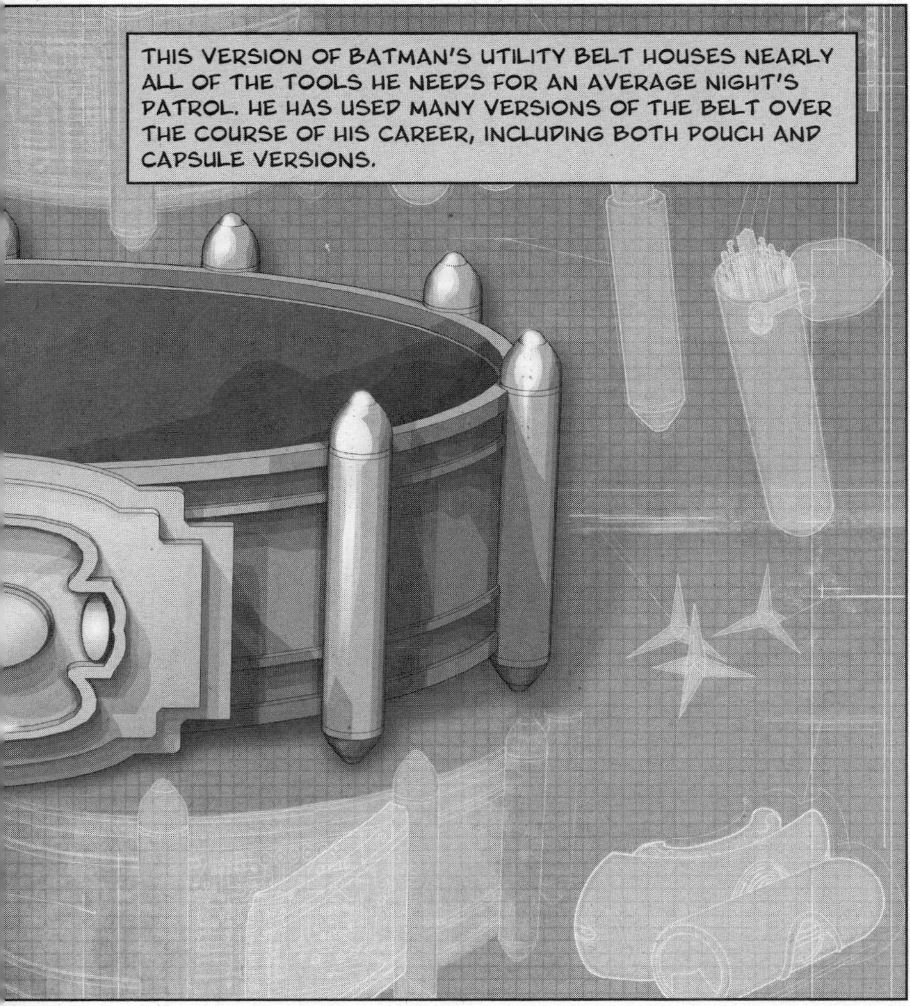
THIS VERSION OF BATMAN'S UTILITY BELT HOUSES NEARLY ALL OF THE TOOLS HE NEEDS FOR AN AVERAGE NIGHT'S PATROL. HE HAS USED MANY VERSIONS OF THE BELT OVER THE COURSE OF HIS CAREER, INCLUDING BOTH POUCH AND CAPSULE VERSIONS.

The grapnel raises Batman into the air in a dramatic fashion and at incredible speeds. The grapnel has not only helped Batman get out of many tough scrapes, but it also adds to the urban legend that the Caped Crusader is a winged creature of the night.

The Batarang was one of Batman's earliest tools, and remains a favorite to this day. Stored in his Utility Belt, Batarangs range from small throwing darts to larger weapons that function like a boomerang. Batman has even developed explosive and remote-controlled varieties.

It soon became clear to the Dark Knight that he would need a quicker way to get around Gotham City. He first employed a Batcycle, a motorcycle equipped for fast speeds and heavily armored against gunfire. For air travel, he used a hang glider in the shape of

BATMAN'S BATCYCLE IS PERFECT FOR GETTING AROUND GOTHAM CITY'S MANY ALLEYWAYS AND ALL THE SMALL PLACES THAT THE BATMOBILE CANNOT GO.

large batwings. Batman later upped the ante with vehicles like his Batmobile, Batboat, Bat-Gyro, and Batwing.

The Batmobile is perhaps the most recognizable of Batman's various vehicles. It is built for speed and protection. The car offers a perfect way for getting from the Batcave to Gotham City in just a few short

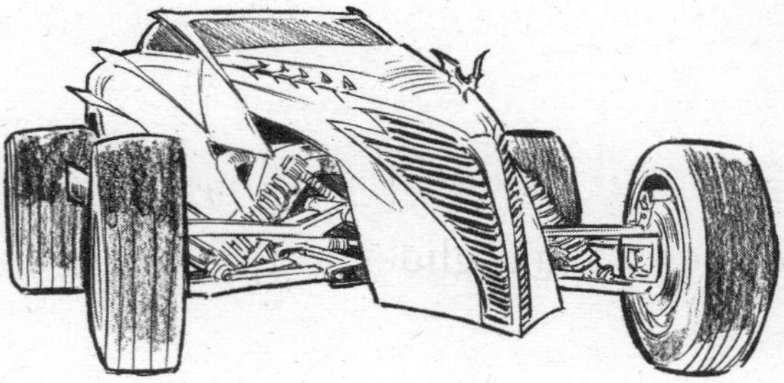

BATMAN MAINTAINS MANY DIFFERENT MODELS OF THE BATMOBILE. THIS ALLOWS HIM TO PICK THE PERFECT CAR TO SUIT EACH OF HIS MISSIONS.

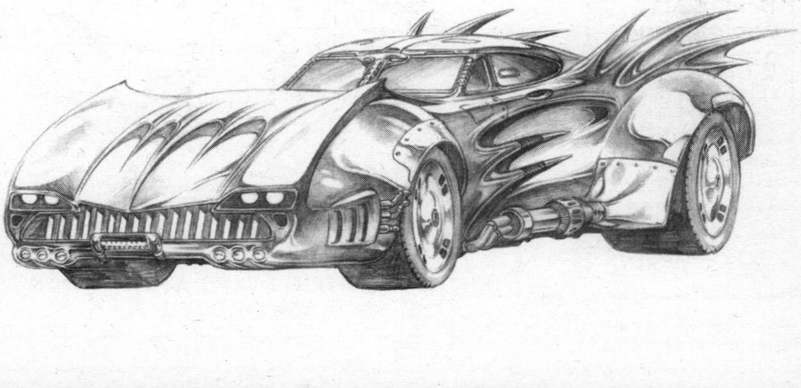

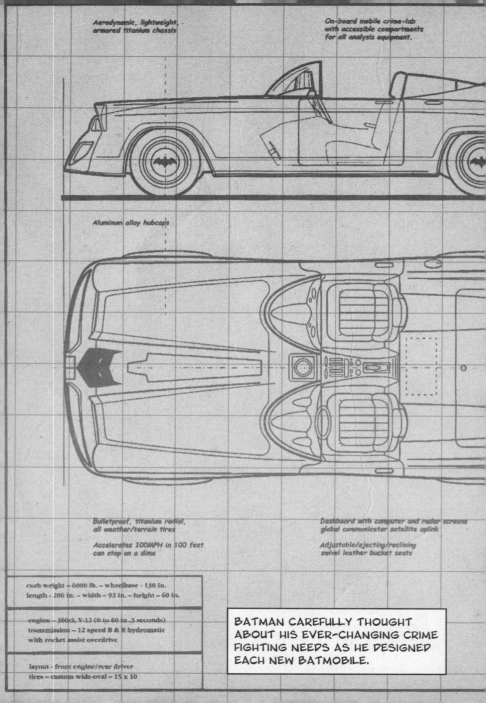

Aerodynamic, lightweight, armored titanium chassis

On-board mobile crime-lab with accessible compartments for all analysis equipment.

Aluminum alloy hubcaps

Bulletproof, titanium radial, all weather/terrain tires

Accelerates 100MPH in 100 feet can stop on a dime

Dashboard with computer and radar screens global communicator satellite uplink

Adjustable/ejecting/reclining swivel leather bucket seats

curb weight – 6000 lb. – wheelbase - 150 in.
length - 200 in. – width - 92 in. – height - 60 in.

engine – 360ci, V-12 (0 to 60 in .3 seconds)
transmission – 12 speed B & R hydromatic
with rocket assist overdrive

layout - front engine/rear driver
tires - custom wide-oval – 15 x 10

BATMAN CAREFULLY THOUGHT ABOUT HIS EVER-CHANGING CRIME FIGHTING NEEDS AS HE DESIGNED EACH NEW BATMOBILE.

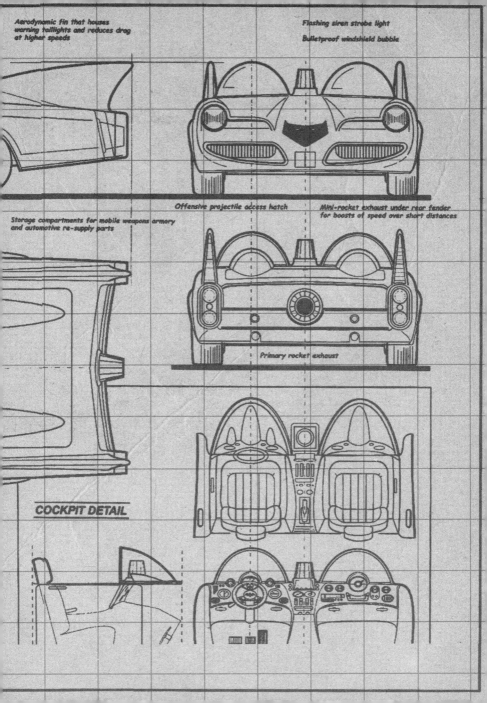

Aerodynamic fin that houses warning taillights and reduces drag at higher speeds

Flashing siren strobe light

Bulletproof windshield bubble

Offensive projectile access hatch

Mini-rocket exhaust under rear fender for boosts of speed over short distances

Storage compartments for mobile weapons armory and automotive re-supply parts

Primary rocket exhaust

COCKPIT DETAIL

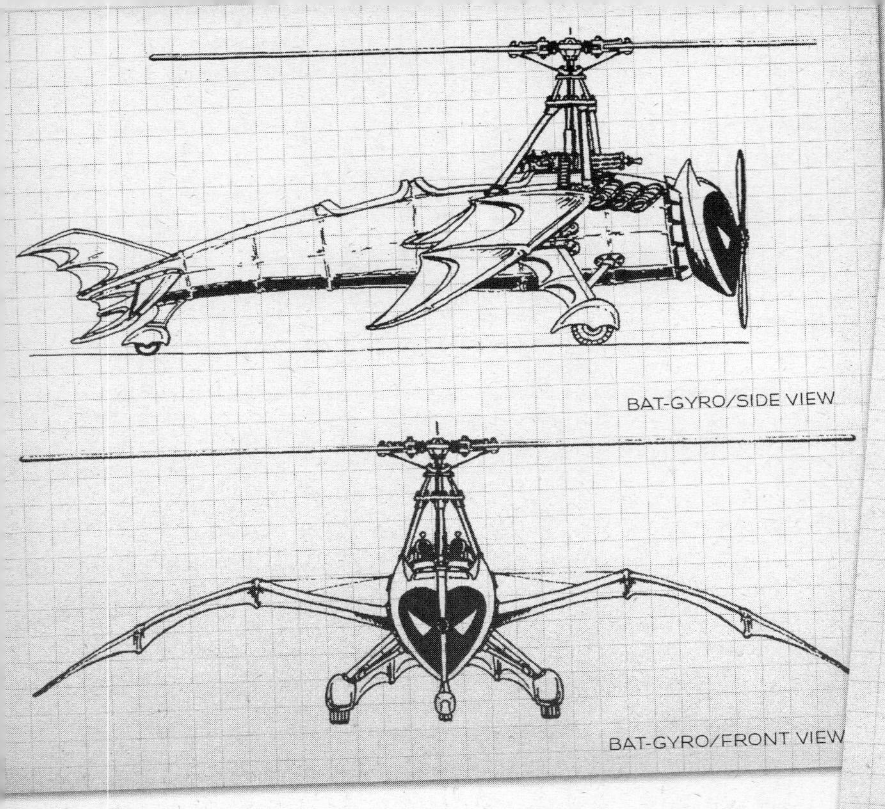
BAT-GYRO/SIDE VIEW
BAT-GYRO/FRONT VIEW

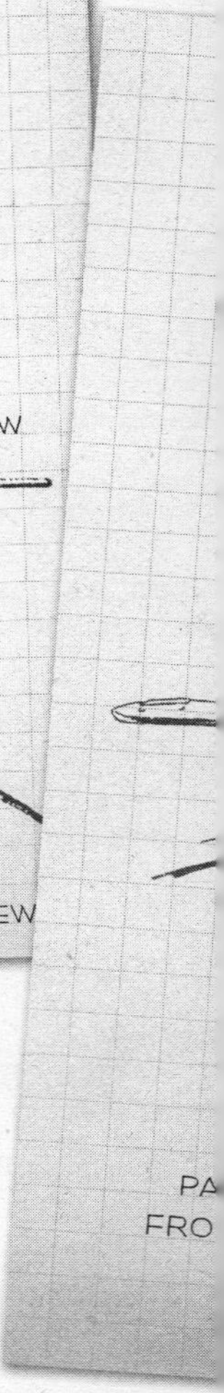

minutes. Batman is constantly tinkering with this vehicle, and has gone through dozens of models over the years. Each is an improvement on the one that came before.

While his hang glider is quiet and effective, Batman often needs a quicker way to travel by air, especially when going long distances. His Bat-Gyro was his earliest attempt at creating an aircraft

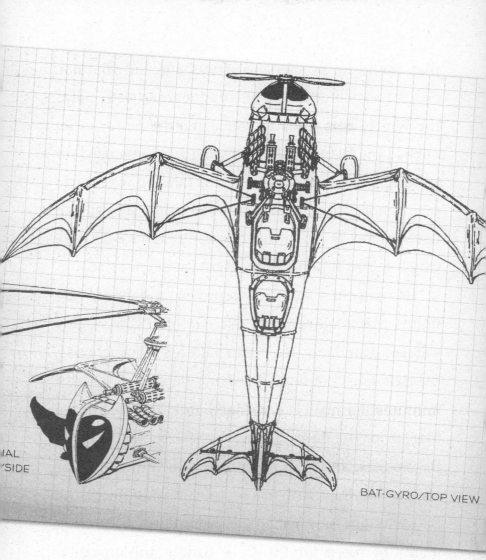

IAL
/SIDE

BAT-GYRO/TOP VIEW

THE BAT-GYRO WAS ONE OF BATMAN'S EARLIEST VEHICLES.
IT WAS LATER REDESIGNED AS THE SLEEKER BATCOPTER, AS
WELL AS THE MUCH SMALLER WHIRLY-BAT.

that would be as silent as it was efficient. Batman created a smaller model of this copter as well, called the Whirly-Bat. He later concocted the powerful jet dubbed the Batwing. The Batwing is mostly used for travel outside of Gotham City, as landing it requires much more space than a crowded urban setting can usually offer. It can fly much faster than his Bat-Gyro, which makes it perfect for international missions.

Batman has even constructed a Batboat for nights that require travel over Gotham City's many waterways or out on the ocean. Like his other vehicles, the Batboat is housed in Batman's Batcave. A massive cavern underneath Wayne Manor, the Batcave offers a hangar for the Batwing, a garage for Batman's many Batmobiles, and even an underground river to enter and exit the Dark Knight's secret lair via Batboat. The Batcave is the perfect home base for Batman, offering plenty of room for the Dark Knight to constantly develop new and improved weapons in his never-ending battle against crime.

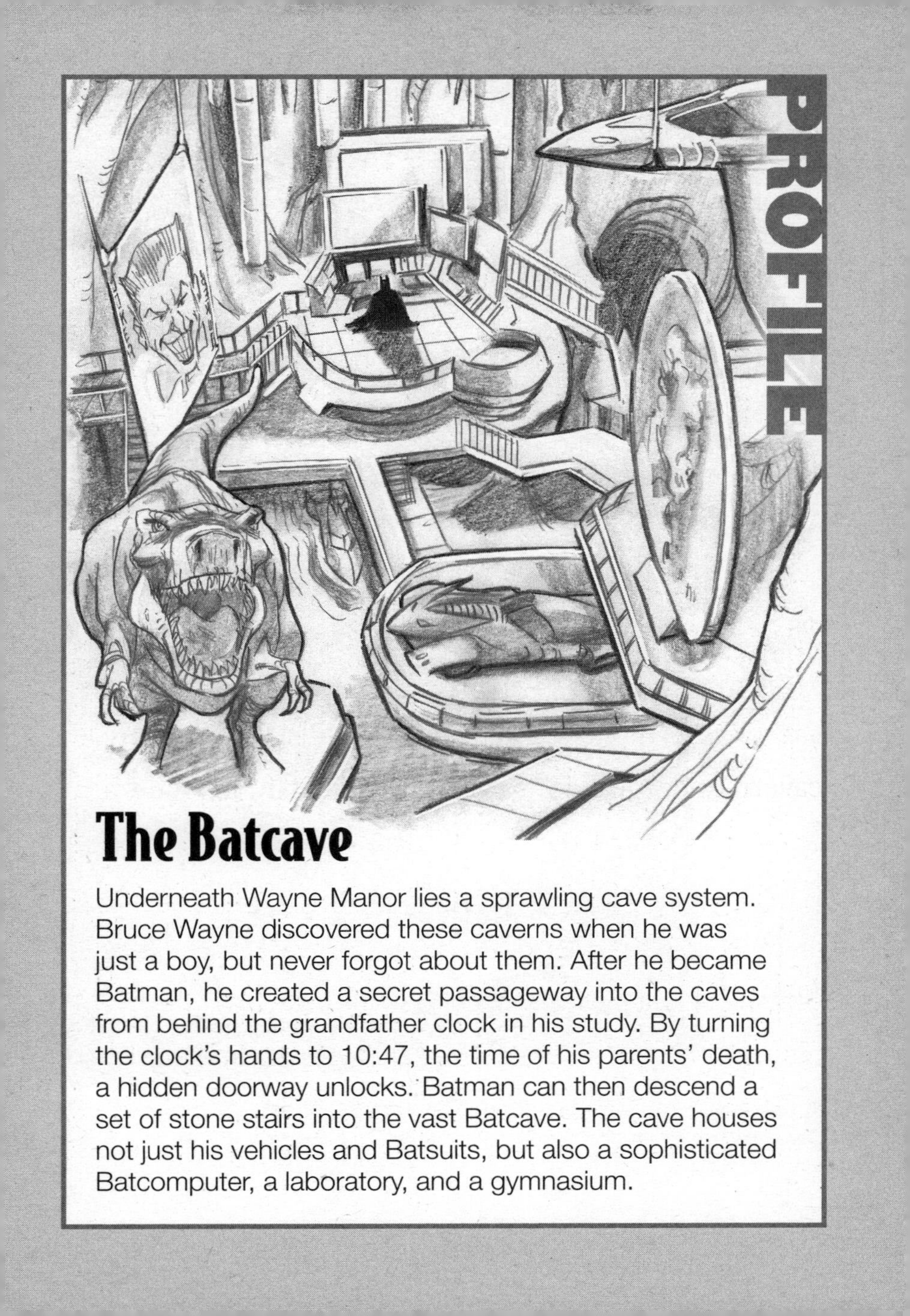

PROFILE

The Batcave

Underneath Wayne Manor lies a sprawling cave system. Bruce Wayne discovered these caverns when he was just a boy, but never forgot about them. After he became Batman, he created a secret passageway into the caves from behind the grandfather clock in his study. By turning the clock's hands to 10:47, the time of his parents' death, a hidden doorway unlocks. Batman can then descend a set of stone stairs into the vast Batcave. The cave houses not just his vehicles and Batsuits, but also a sophisticated Batcomputer, a laboratory, and a gymnasium.

BATMAN USES
HIS BATBOAT
FOR QUICK
TRAVEL ALONG
GOTHAM
CITY'S THREE
MAIN WATER-
WAYS:
THE GOTHAM,
THE SPRANG,
AND THE
FINGER RIVER.

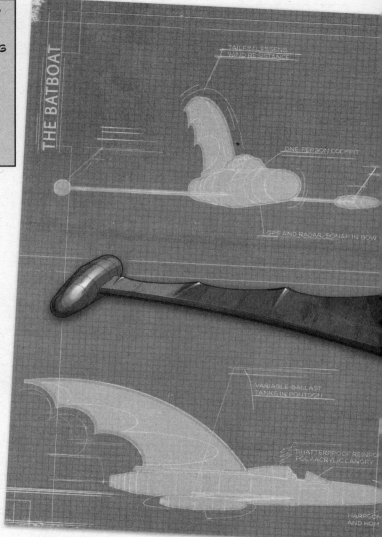

THE BATBOAT

TAIL FIN LESSENS
WIND RESISTANCE

ONE-PERSON COCKPIT

GPS AND RADAR/SONAR IN BOW

VARIABLE BALLAST
TANKS IN PONTOON

SHATTERPROOF REINFO
POLYACRYLIC CANOPY

HARPOON
AND HOM

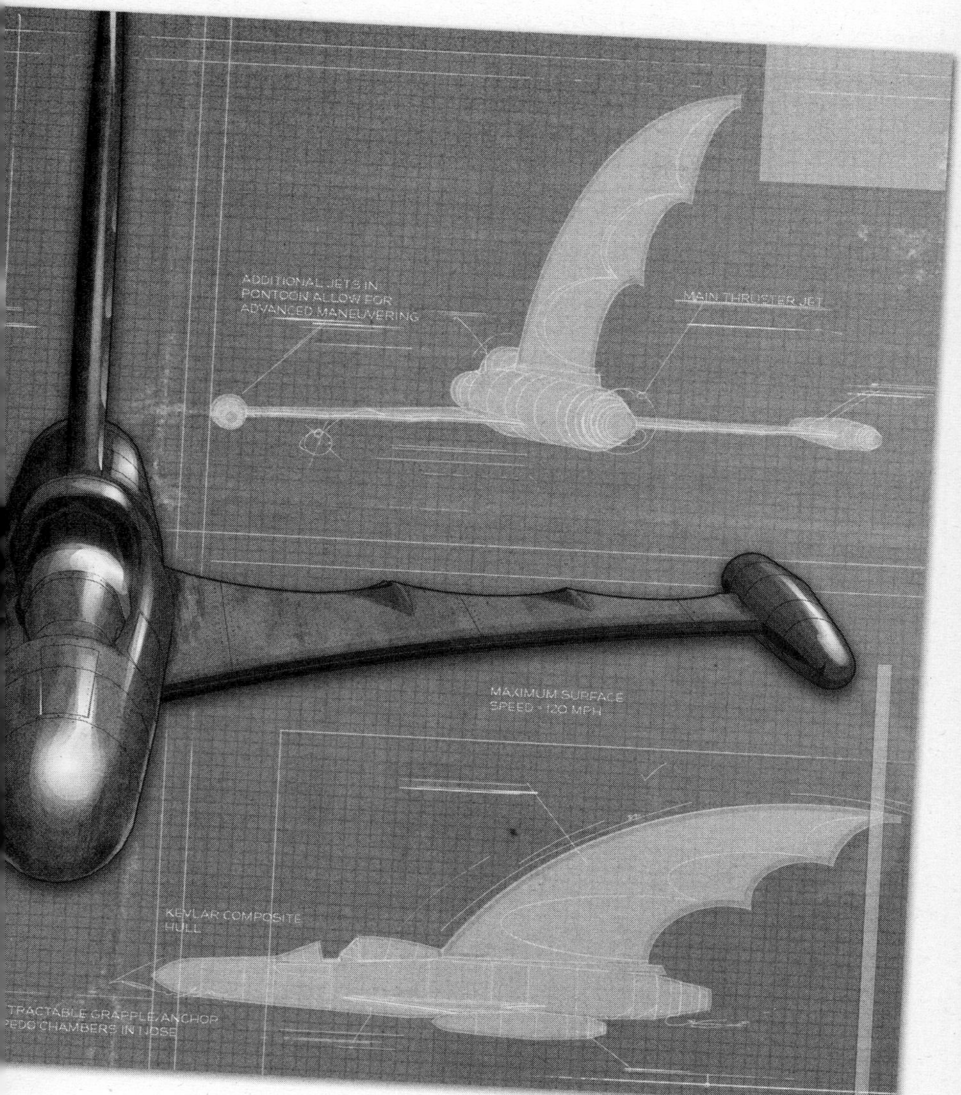
ADDITIONAL JETS IN PONTOON ALLOW FOR ADVANCED MANEUVERING
MAIN THRUSTER JET
MAXIMUM SURFACE SPEED = 120 MPH
KEVLAR COMPOSITE HULL
TRACTABLE GRAPPLE/ANCHOR
PEDO CHAMBERS IN NOSE

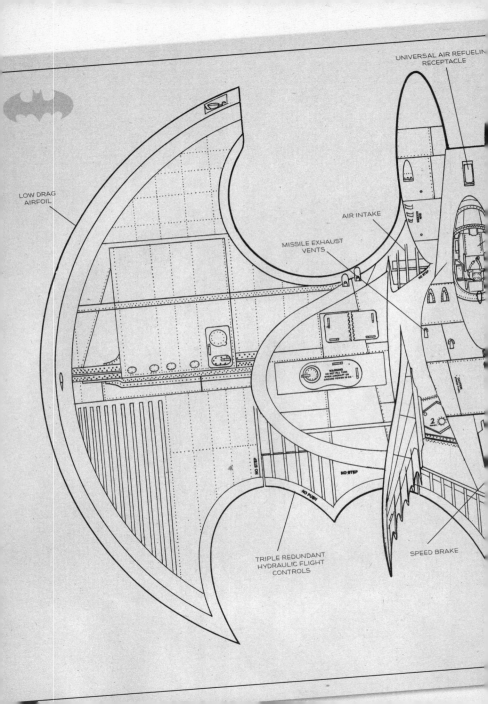

UNIVERSAL AIR REFUELING
RECEPTACLE

LOW DRAG
AIRFOIL

AIR INTAKE

MISSILE EXHAUST
VENTS

WARNING
DO NOT FILL TANK
WHEN AIRCRAFT ON
GROUND POWER IS ON

NO STEP

NO STEP

NO PUSH

TRIPLE REDUNDANT
HYDRAULIC FLIGHT
CONTROLS

SPEED BRAKE

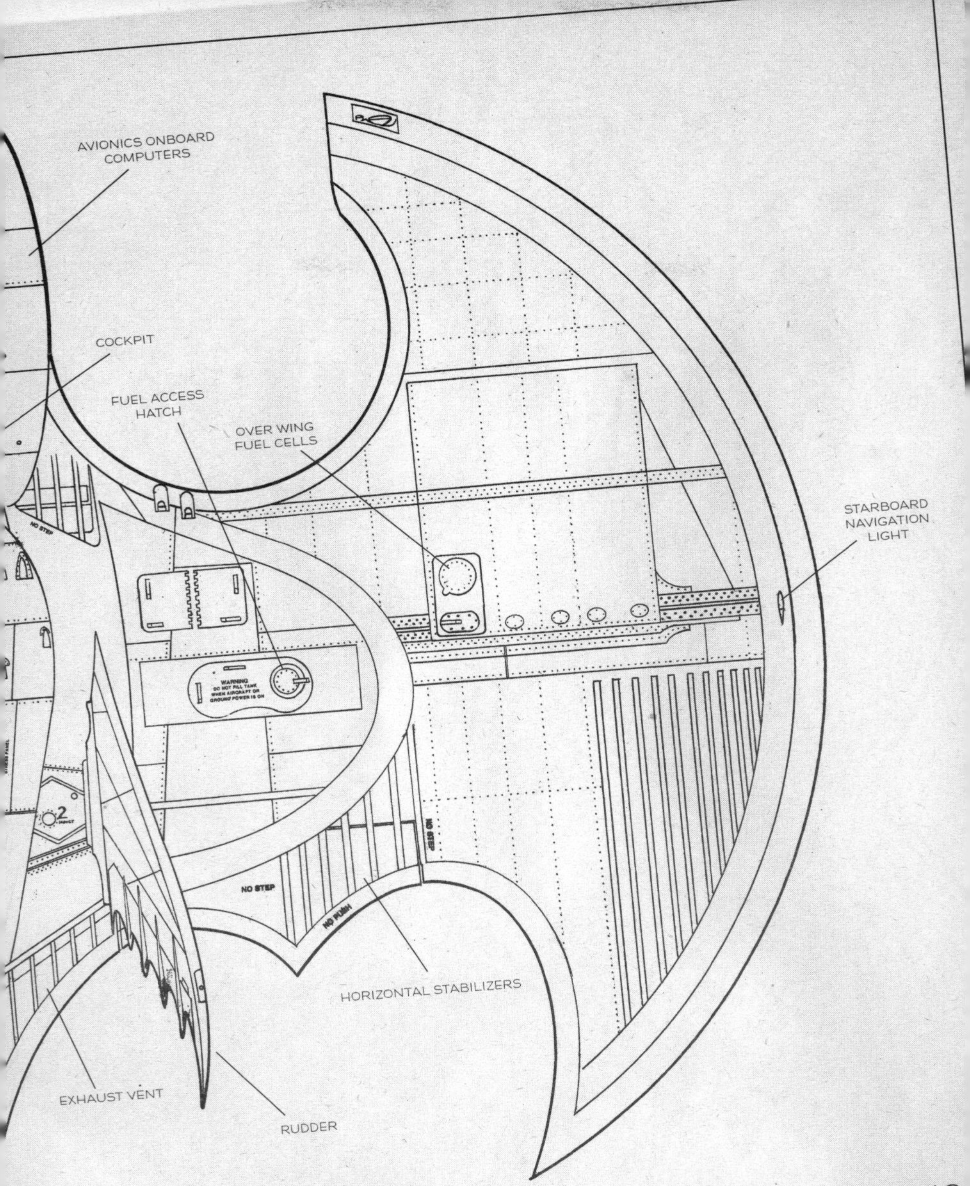
AVIONICS ONBOARD COMPUTERS
COCKPIT
FUEL ACCESS HATCH
OVER WING FUEL CELLS
STARBOARD NAVIGATION LIGHT
WARNING
DO NOT FILL TANK WHEN AIRCRAFT OR GROUND POWER IS ON
NO STEP
NO STEP
NO PUSH
HORIZONTAL STABILIZERS
EXHAUST VENT
RUDDER

THE BATWING

THE BATWING REMAINS ONE OF BATMAN'S FASTEST FORMS OF TRANSPORTATION. IT CAN BE FLOWN BY TRADITIONAL PILOTING TECHNIQUES OR EVEN BY REMOTE CONTROL.

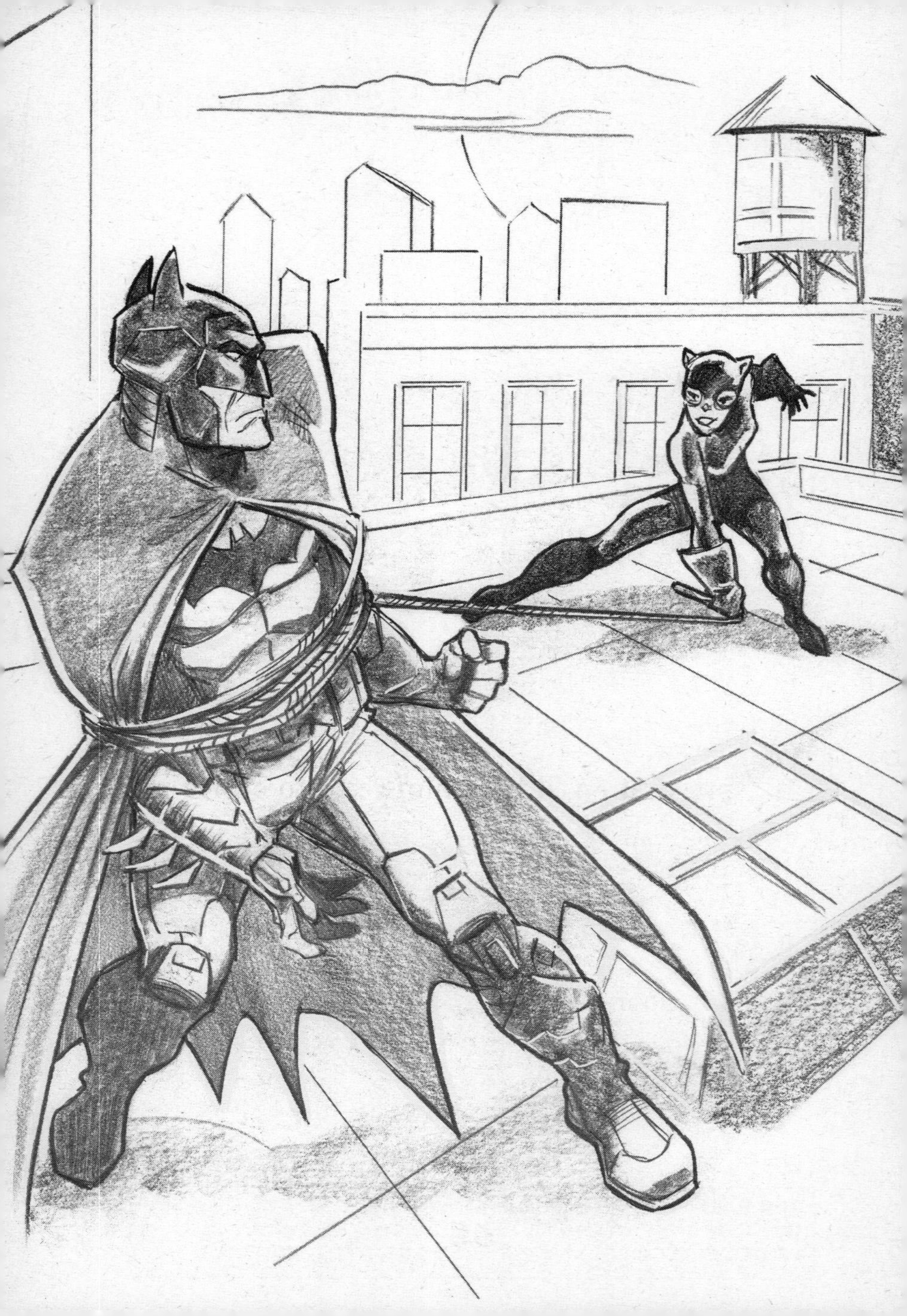

CHAPTER FOUR

LEARNING CURVE

Bruce Wayne had trained nearly his entire life to become Batman. Even with all of that preparation, it took him years to evolve into the efficient crime fighter he is today. Becoming a Super Hero isn't an exact science. It required much trial and error. And Gotham City certainly offered up its fair share of trials for the Caped Crusader to overcome.

There are many that say that Gotham City attracts a certain type of crazed personality. Others insist that Batman attracts the very villains he is forced to combat. But no matter which theory is correct, Batman continues to face dozens of bizarre criminals.

The most notorious of those villains is the Joker. When Batman was just beginning his career, he was viewed as a mysterious creature of the night. So on the night he confronted the criminal called the Red Hood at the ACE Chemical Factory, his appearance

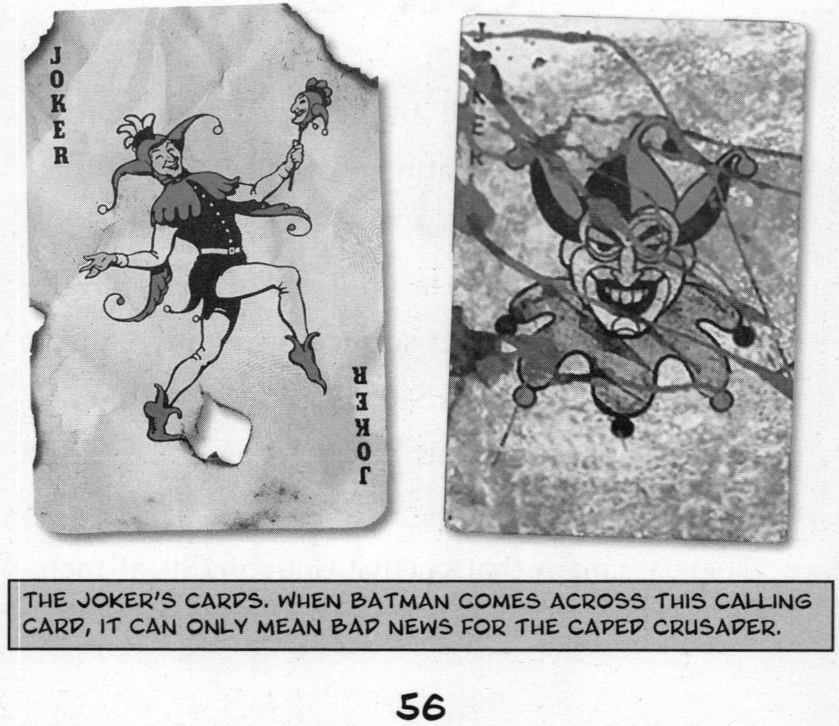
JOKER
JOKER

THE JOKER'S CARDS. WHEN BATMAN COMES ACROSS THIS CALLING CARD, IT CAN ONLY MEAN BAD NEWS FOR THE CAPED CRUSADER.

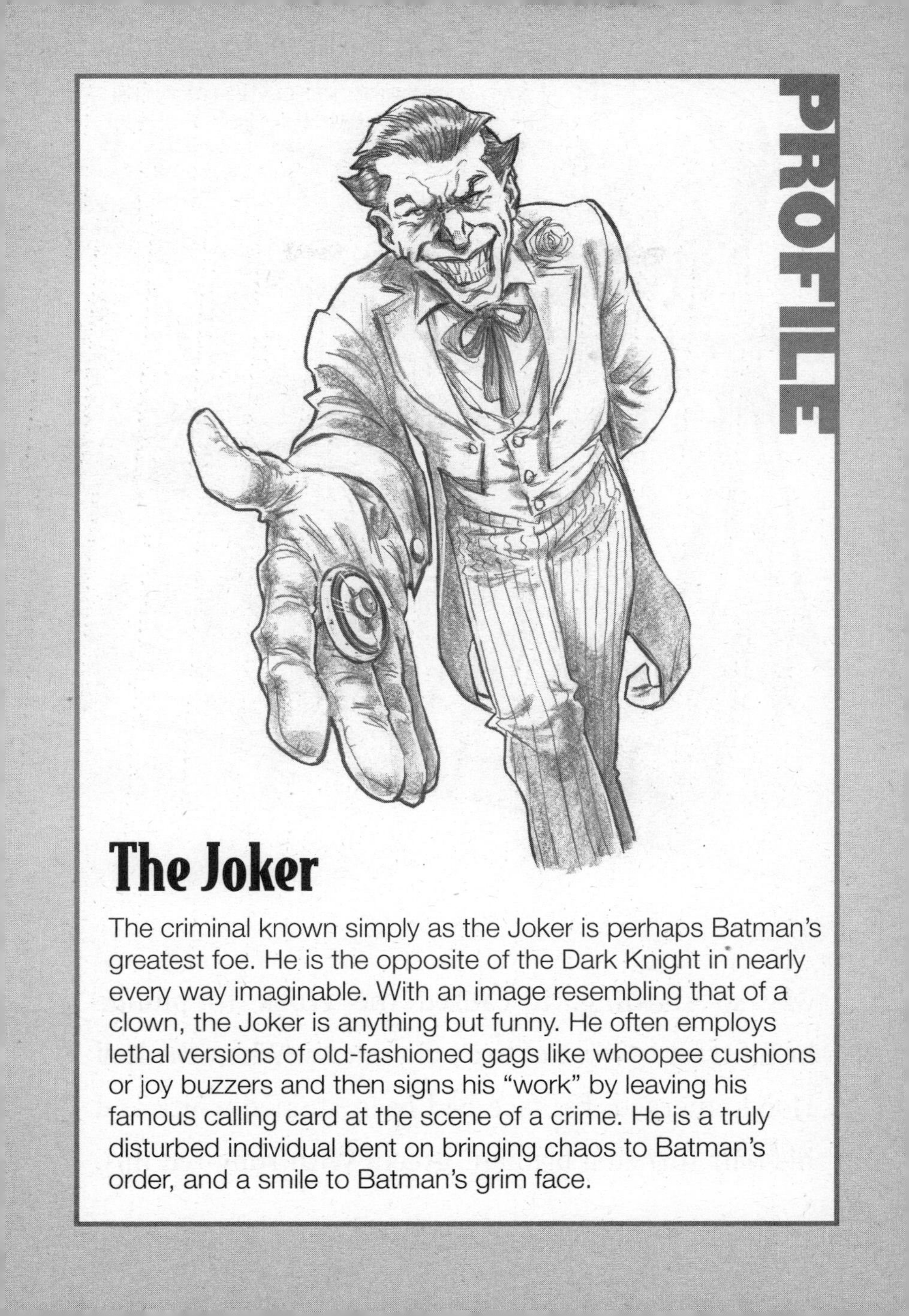

PROFILE

The Joker

The criminal known simply as the Joker is perhaps Batman's greatest foe. He is the opposite of the Dark Knight in nearly every way imaginable. With an image resembling that of a clown, the Joker is anything but funny. He often employs lethal versions of old-fashioned gags like whoopee cushions or joy buzzers and then signs his "work" by leaving his famous calling card at the scene of a crime. He is a truly disturbed individual bent on bringing chaos to Batman's order, and a smile to Batman's grim face.

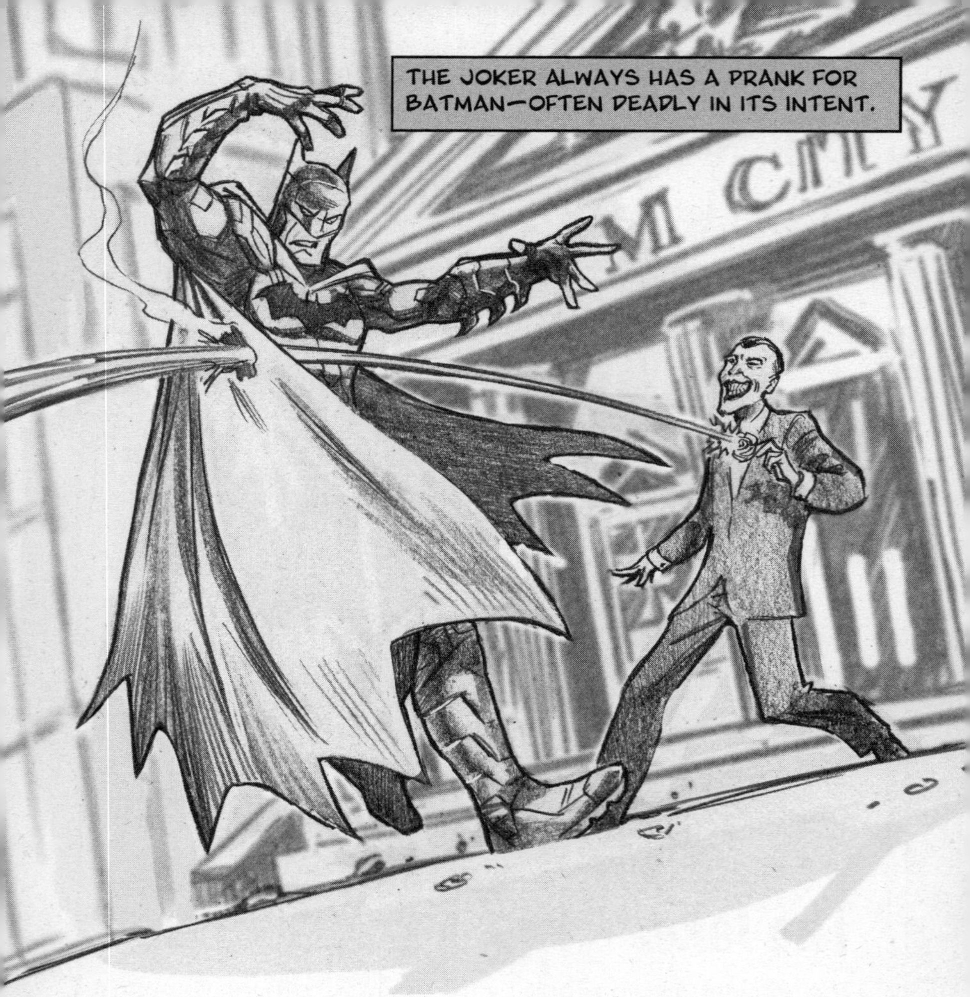
THE JOKER ALWAYS HAS A PRANK FOR BATMAN—OFTEN DEADLY IN ITS INTENT.

was so startling, it caused the crook to plunge headfirst into a vat of toxic chemicals. When the Red Hood emerged, his face had been stained white and his hair turned a brilliant green. With ruby-red lips, there was nothing left for the Red Hood to do but smile. And he hasn't stopped smiling since.

It took some time before Batman linked the Red Hood to the insane new villain calling himself the Joker. And while his true identity has never been discovered, the Joker has created quite a legacy for himself. From his equally disturbed sidekick, Harley Quinn, to his many campaigns to poison or otherwise harm the citizens of Gotham City, the Joker's true goals often remain a secret only known to himself.

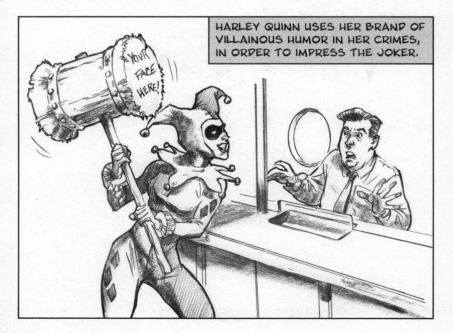

HARLEY QUINN USES HER BRAND OF VILLAINOUS HUMOR IN HER CRIMES, IN ORDER TO IMPRESS THE JOKER.

Catwoman was another criminal Batman met when he was starting out in Gotham City. Selina Kyle donned a similar costume to Batman's and began traversing Gotham City's rooftops. A cat-o'-nine-tails

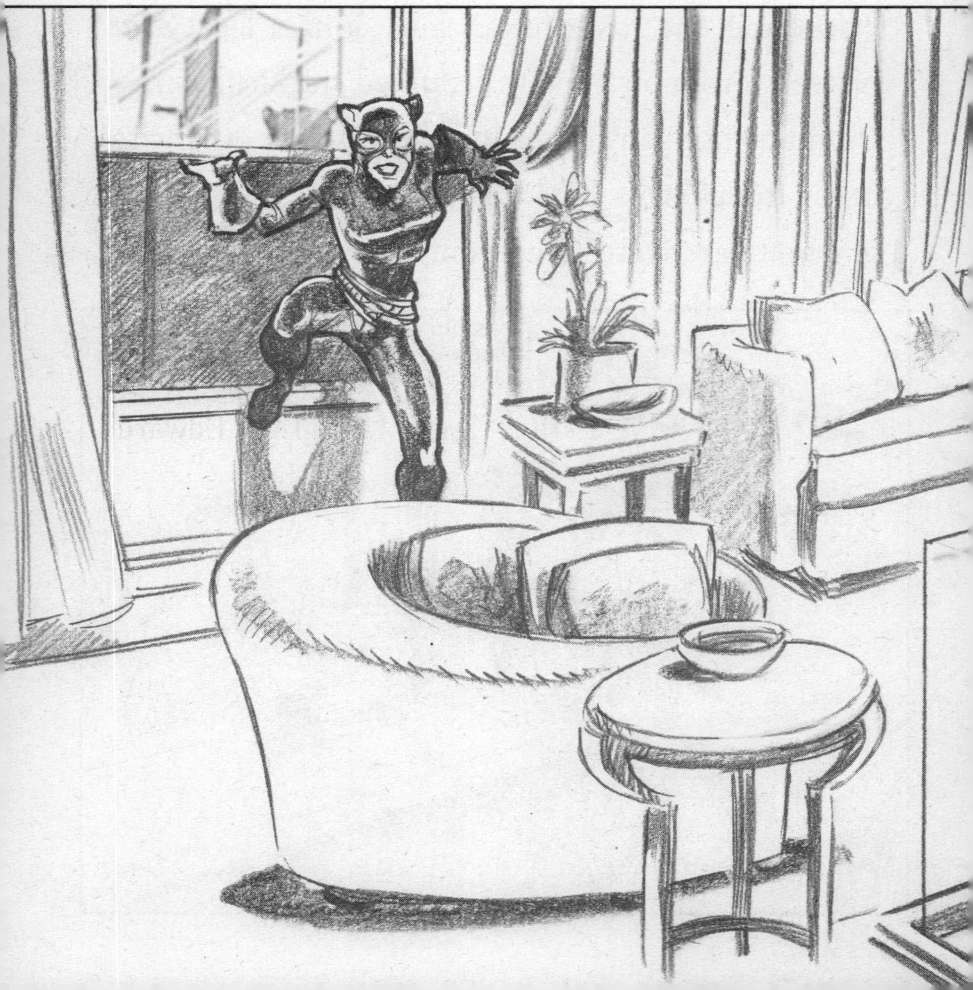

is her weapon of choice, and cat-themed valuables are often the targets of her robberies. However, unlike the Joker, Catwoman has shown a moral side. She has often helped Batman on a case when it benefits her or

her own neighborhood. While Batman can't completely trust her, Catwoman has helped the citizens of Gotham City's East End too many times to count.

The Riddler's criminal career was in part inspired by the idea of challenging the Dark Knight. Edward Nygma loved the concept of brainteasers ever since he was a child cheating at puzzles in school. He began a life of crime and adopted the name the Riddler when he realized that the only thing he was

THE RIDDLER'S CANE WAS DESIGNED WITH A QUESTION MARK-SHAPED HANDLE AND SEVERAL BUTTONS THAT OPERATE REMOTE DEATHTRAPS SPREAD THROUGHOUT HIS HIDEOUT.

truly good at was cheating the system. He'd send the Gotham City Police Department riddles to solve before committing his crimes. Unfortunately, they couldn't solve them. But Batman was able to not only deduce the Riddler's schemes, he was able to thwart those same crimes. Even though this resulted in the

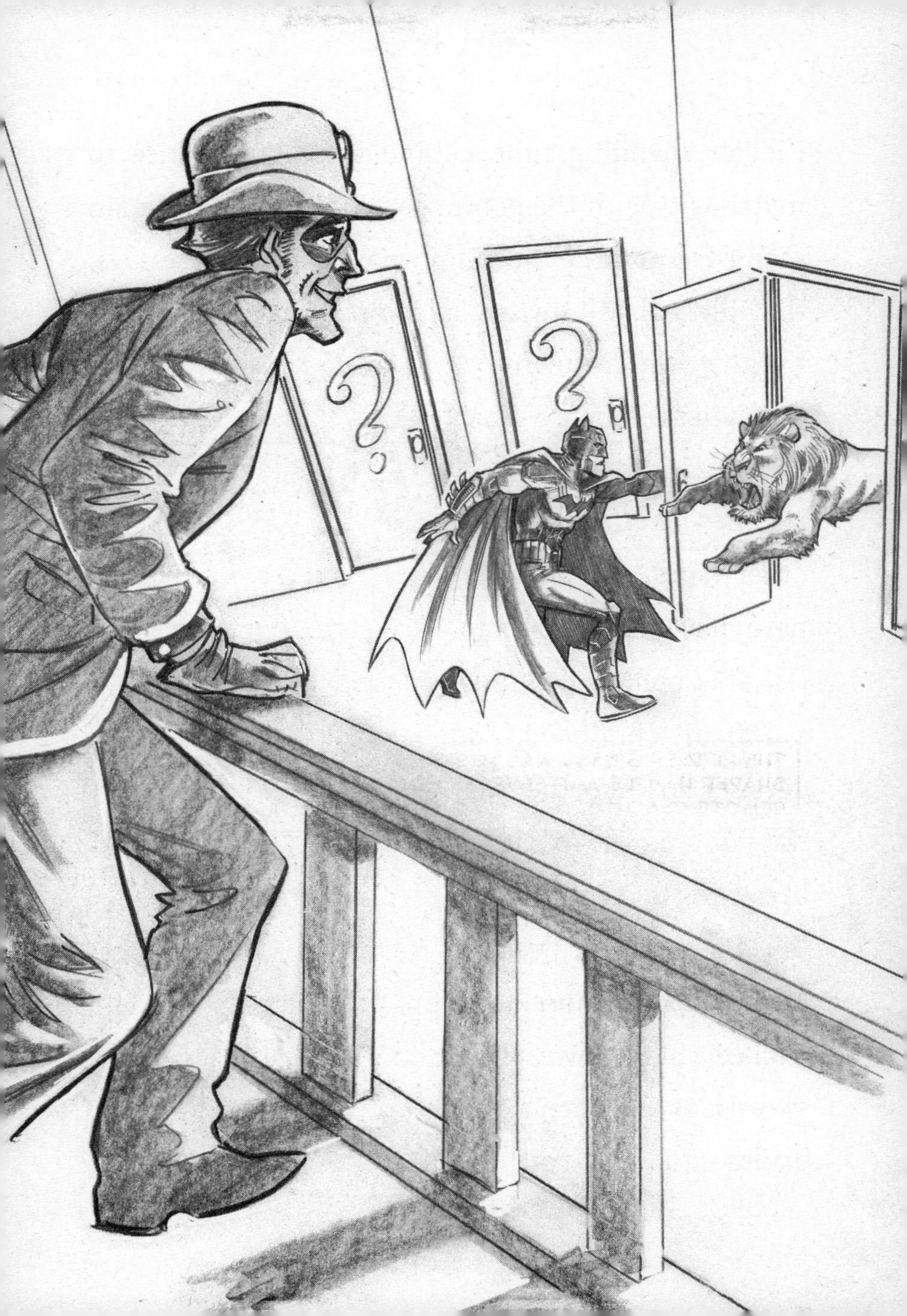

Riddler spending time behind bars, the chance to match wits with the genius-level intellect of Batman seemed to give the Riddler purpose in life. These days, the criminal still thrives on competing with the Dark Knight, but Batman has no patience for Nygma's games.

The Penguin, on the other hand, would rather have never met Batman. Oswald Cobblepot suffered a difficult childhood, and decided to take the easy way out as an adult by becoming a criminal. As the Penguin, he uses a host of deadly umbrellas— tricked out with weapons, swords, or even helicopter blades—to pull off his

crimes. He soon decided it would be more profitable to be behind the scenes. So he worked his way up the criminal ladder to become one of the underworld's most notorious crime bosses. The Penguin runs the

70
66
60
56
50
46
40
36

AT FIRST GLANCE, THE PENGUIN APPEARS HARMLESS. HOWEVER UNDERNEATH HIS ALMOST COMICAL EXTERIOR IS THE BRAIN OF A RUTHLESS CRIMINAL GENIUS.

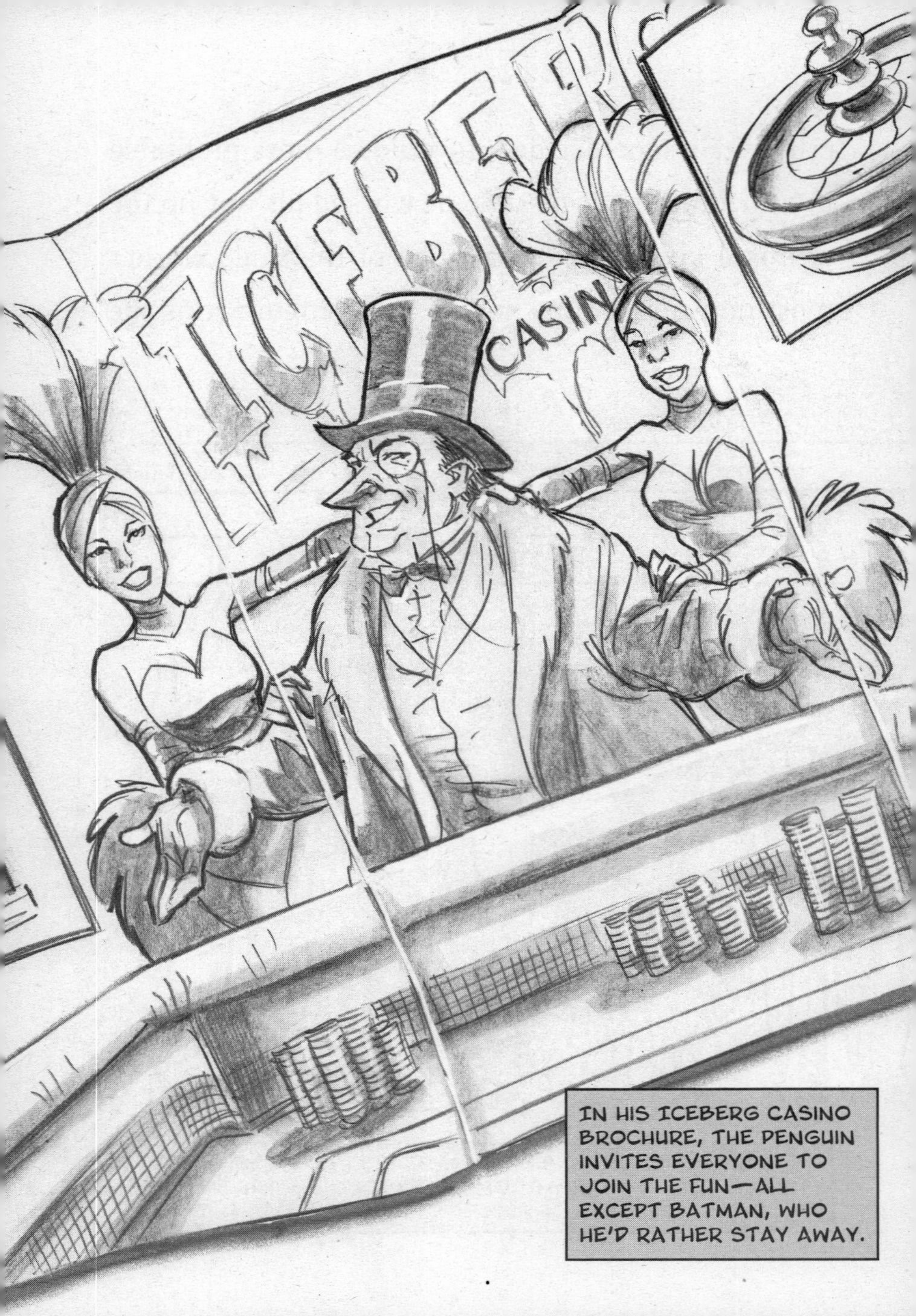
IN HIS ICEBERG CASINO BROCHURE, THE PENGUIN INVITES EVERYONE TO JOIN THE FUN—ALL EXCEPT BATMAN, WHO HE'D RATHER STAY AWAY.

the Iceberg Casino, a popular nightclub. Batman often pays the club a late-night visit, forcing the Penguin to give him information on the latest activities of Gotham City's underworld. When threatened with the imposing figure of the Dark Knight, the Penguin has no choice but to comply.

Not all of Batman's foes started out as enemies. His old friend Harvey Dent from preparatory school was a friend to both Bruce Wayne and Batman before he was scarred by acid from an irate criminal. When half of his handsome features were ruined, Harvey's

HARVEY DENT'S DOUBLE-SIDED COIN WAS HIS GOOD-LUCK CHARM. HE SCARRED ONE OF THE HEADS AFTER HE BECAME THE CRIMINAL KNOWN AS TWO-FACE.

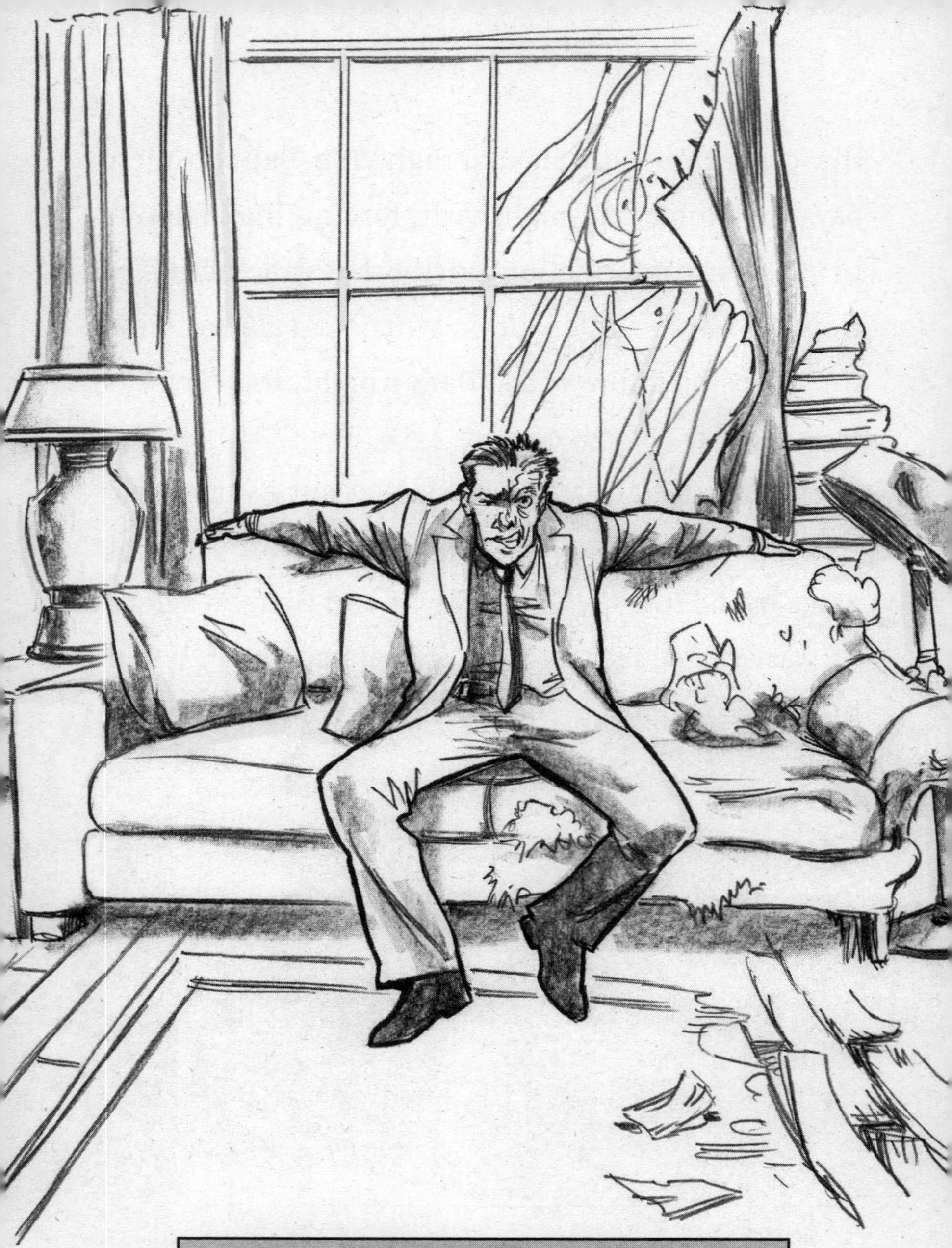

TWO-FACE'S SPLIT PERSONALITY AFFECTS EVERY ASPECT OF HIS LIFE, INCLUDING HIS HIDEOUT.

mind snapped. He developed a split personality as the villain called Two-Face. When Batman was first starting out in Gotham City, Harvey Dent was the city's noble district attorney. He often worked hand in hand with Batman and Commissioner Gordon in their mission to rid the city of crime. Now, as the tragic figure Two-Face, Harvey Dent relies on the flip of a coin to decide between making a good or an evil decision. Unfortunately for Gotham City, the evil side seems to win more times than not, a fact that haunts Bruce Wayne. Bruce wishes nothing more than to see his old friend healed and back on the side of the angels.

Even today, as criminals continue to emerge in Gotham City, Batman is forced to adjust his approach to fighting crime. Each new threat causes him to adapt his techniques. Every case makes him a better hero, and every night brings him a little closer to being the man he has sworn an oath to become.

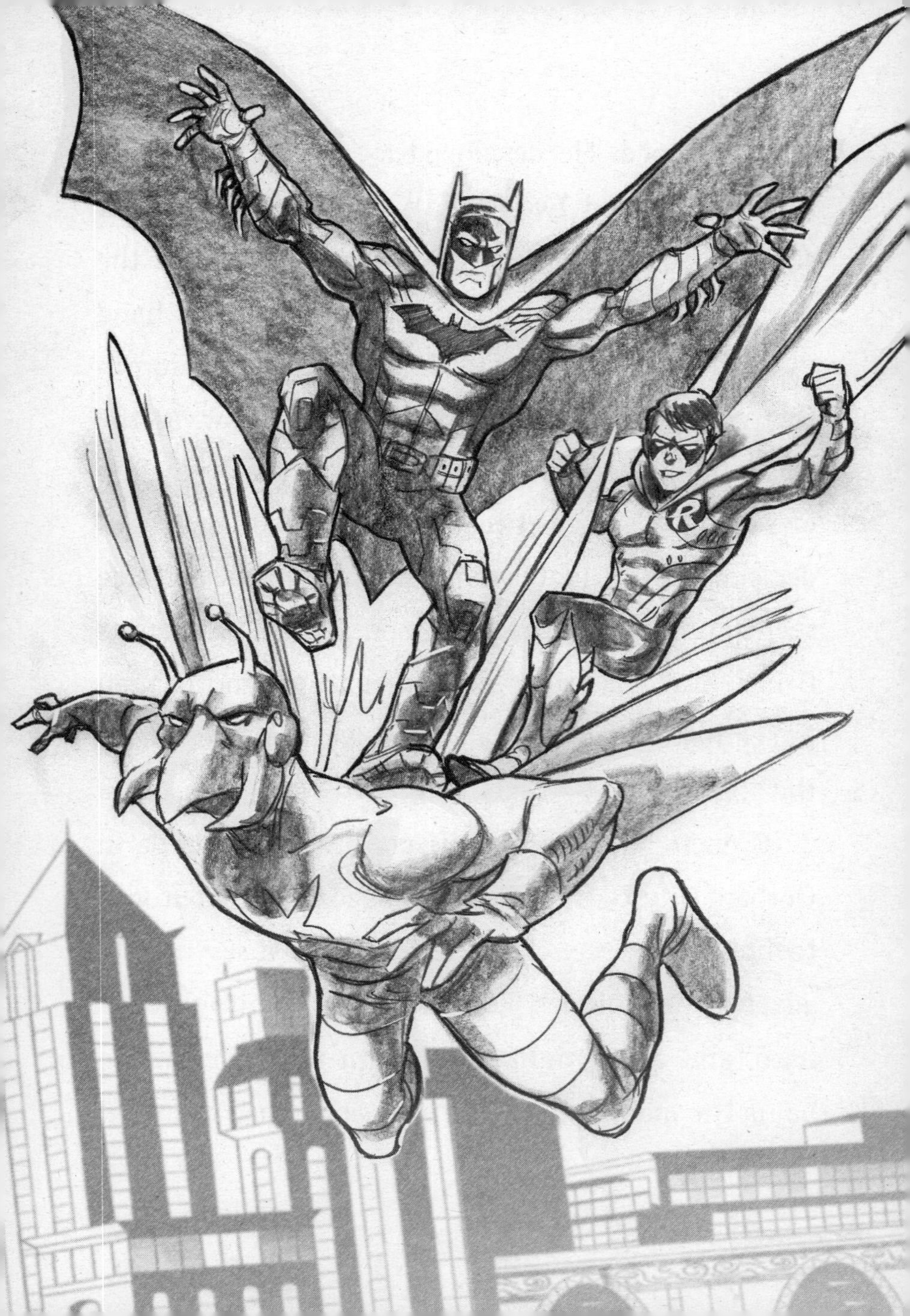

CHAPTER FIVE

THE DYNAMIC DUO

When Bruce Wayne first donned the mantle of Batman, he believed his crusade would be a solitary one. However, that would quickly prove not to be the case. Gotham City has a way of bringing out the worst in people, but it also has a way of forging great heroes. Not the least of which were the many young people who adopted the title of Batman's partner, Robin the Boy Wonder.

The first Robin was Dick Grayson, a former big-top acrobat. Grayson's parents plummeted to their

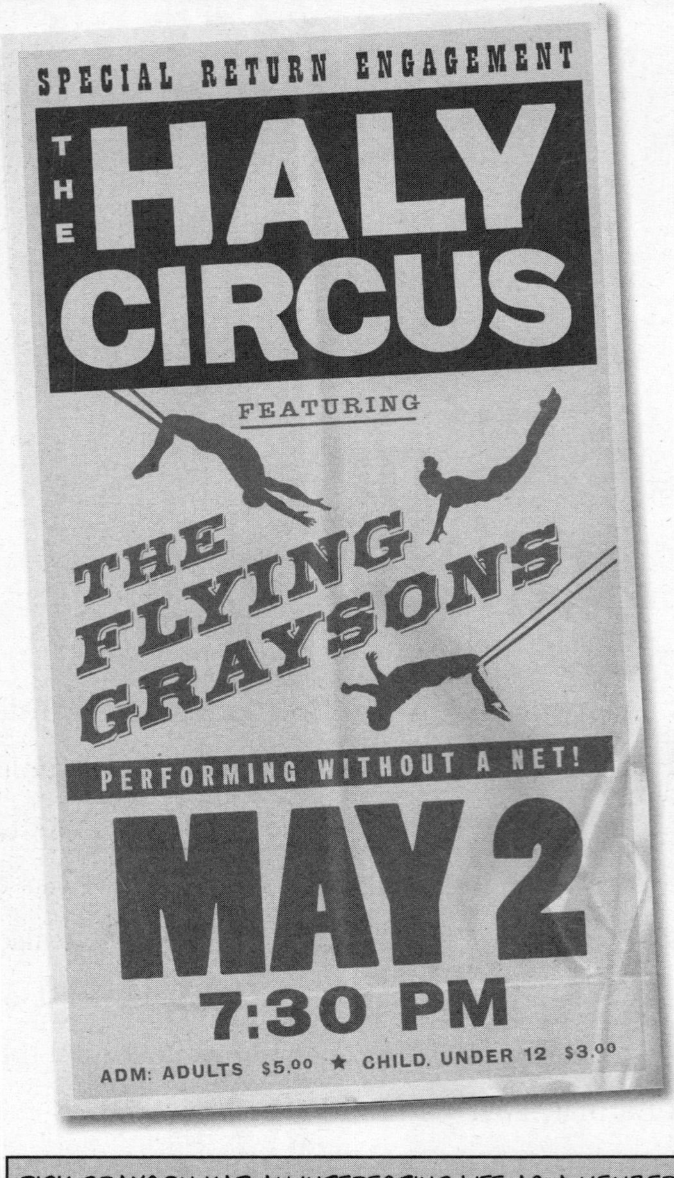
SPECIAL RETURN ENGAGEMENT
THE HALY CIRCUS
FEATURING
THE FLYING GRAYSONS
PERFORMING WITHOUT A NET!
MAY 2
7:30 PM
ADM: ADULTS $5.00 ★ CHILD. UNDER 12 $3.00

DICK GRAYSON HAD AN INTERESTING LIFE AS A MEMBER OF THE HALY CIRCUS. WHEN HE JOINED BATMAN AS HIS PARTNER, HIS LIFE BECAME EVEN MORE EXCITING.

deaths at a Gotham City circus performance, forever changing Dick's life. Bruce Wayne was in the audience on that fateful night. He saw himself in the face of the shattered Dick Grayson, and invited the young man to live at Wayne Manor as his ward. It wasn't long before Dick Grayson learned of Bruce's double life. When Dick realized that his parents had been murdered and had not died in some freak accident, he soon teamed up with Batman to catch his parents'

ROBIN'S ORIGINAL MASK KEPT HIS IDENTITY A SECRET. IT WAS INSPIRED IN PART BY THE LEGEND OF ROBIN HOOD.

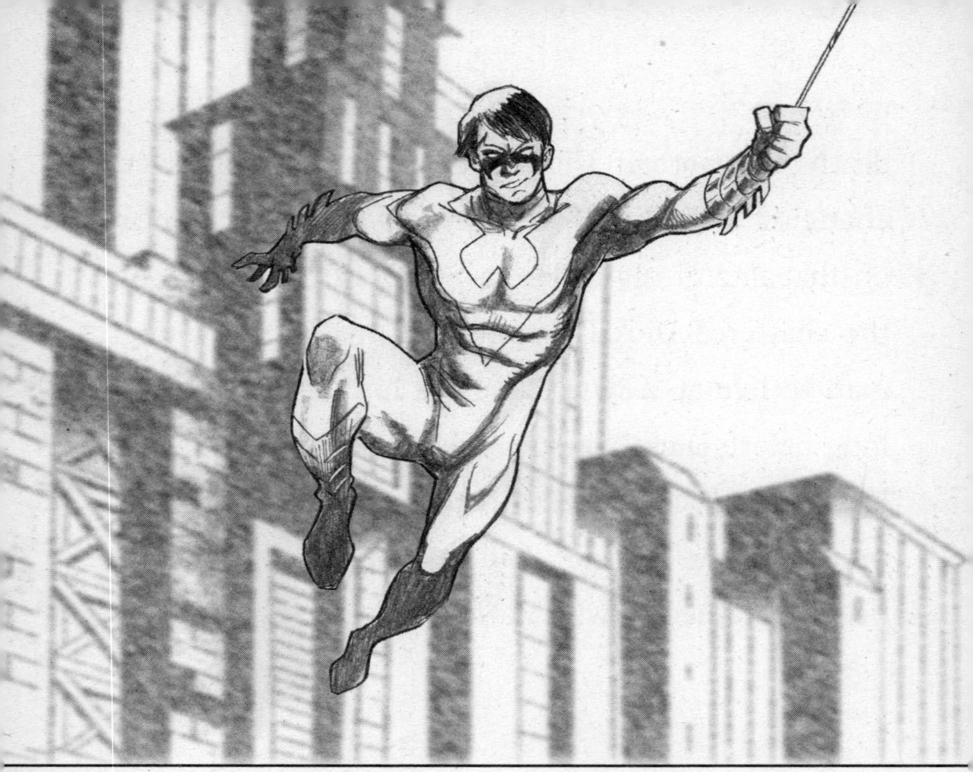

killer. After which, the two formed a partnership that would last for years. They became the Dynamic Duo: Batman and Robin.

When Dick Grayson matured, he set out on his own. He adopted the name Nightwing, and began to fight crime in his unique way.

After Nightwing branched out, Batman adopted a second Robin in the form of Jason Todd. Jason was a street-smart kid who lived the definition of a hard-knock life. He became Bruce Wayne's ward and Batman's partner after impressing the Dark Knight with his boldness and quick thinking. Unfortunately, Jason would soon die at the hands of the Joker. (But fate would bring Jason Todd back after a dip in a mysterious Lazarus Pit. He then became the new Red Hood. He dedicated his life to a more violent style of crime fighting as he dealt with his anger issues.)

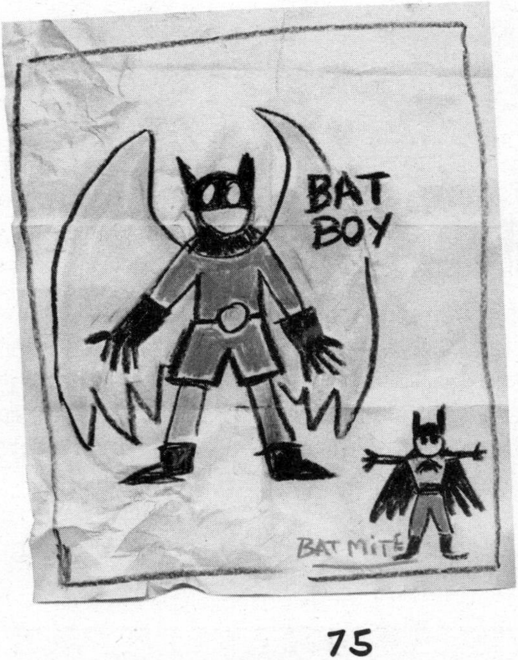
BAT BOY
BAT MITE

A DRAWING OF DICK'S FROM CHILDHOOD.

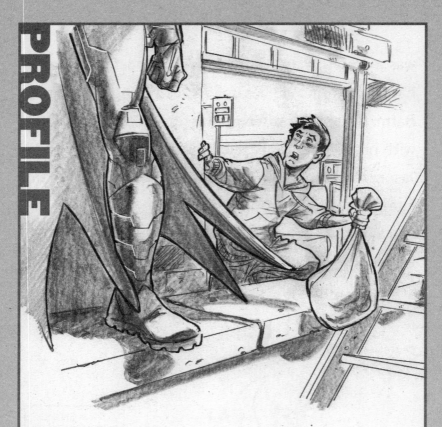

Jason Todd

Born into a life of poverty, Jason Todd's father was a criminal, and his family suffered as a result. Feeling he had no other choice, Jason was set to follow in his father's corrupt footsteps. When Batman first found the boy, Jason was attempting to steal drugs from Dr. Leslie Thompkins's clinic. Seeing a bit of himself in Jason, Batman decided to take the boy under his wing. He focused Jason's anger toward a noble purpose, and soon this misguided young man became the next Robin.

Without a partner, Batman was then pursued by the computer-savvy Tim Drake. Tim was an ambitious young man who, unlike Jason, didn't carry even the slightest bit of a chip on his shoulder. He wanted nothing more than to prove himself as Batman's partner, and worked hard to train his body to be as powerful as his young mind. Batman noticed Tim's persistence and was impressed by the skills of this bright young man. He finally accepted him as the third Robin. Tim later set himself apart from the pack by adopting the name Red Robin.

The current Robin partnering with Batman is Damian Wayne, Bruce Wayne's own son! Damian's mother is Talia al Ghūl, a terrorist who once shared a romance with the Dark Knight. When she felt he was old enough, Talia allowed Damian to meet his father. Batman was originally appalled by Damian's lack of moral character, but knew it was his duty to shape this young boy in the Batman's image. Damian idolized his father and soon abandoned his corrupt

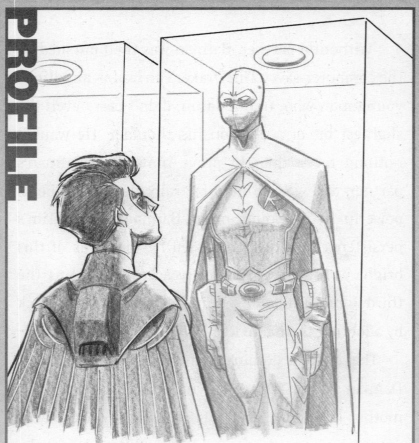

Tim Drake

Perhaps the smartest Robin, Tim Drake made every effort to help the Dark Knight even before he became his partner. His persistence and determination eventually caught Batman's attention. He became the next Robin after the Joker killed Jason Todd. Just as Jason would later be brought back to life, Tim would also evolve. He took the name Red Robin as a symbol of his own individuality.

mother to become Batman's newest partner. This new Robin has a lot to prove, but Batman is working to teach the young man discipline and respect. Meanwhile, Damian constantly surprises the Dark

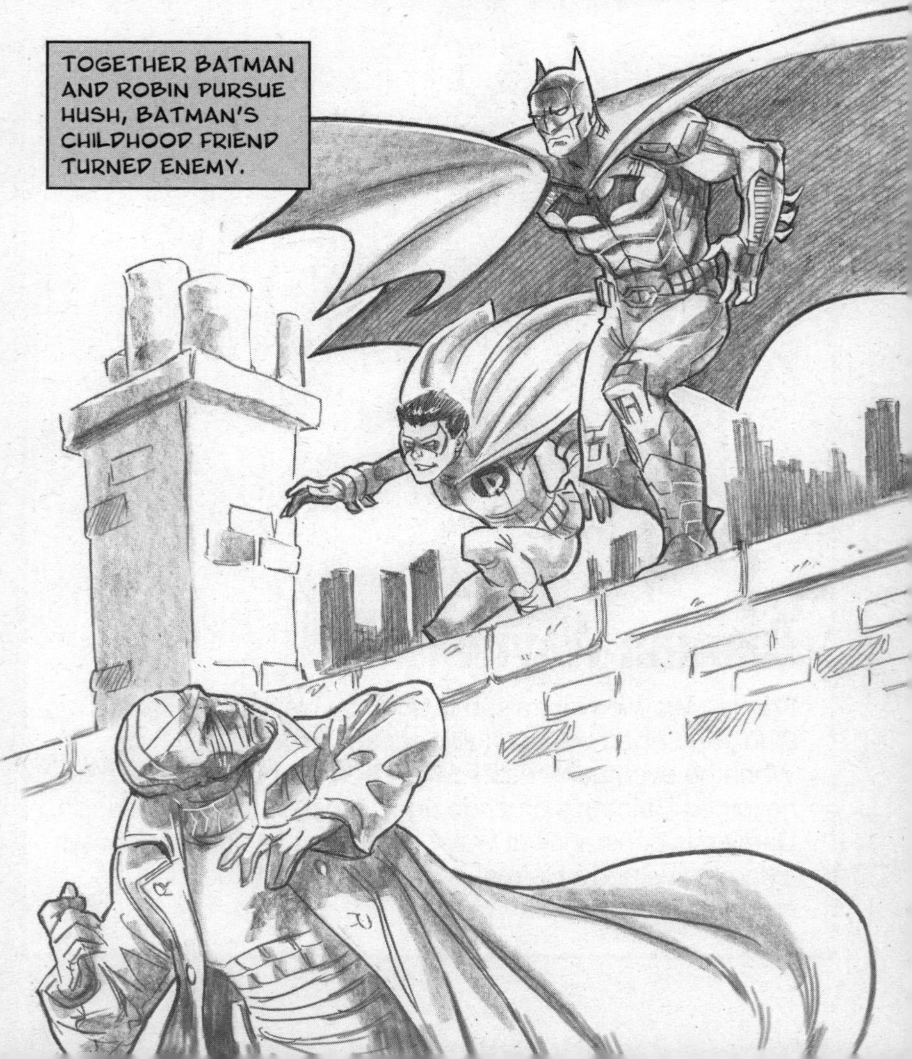
TOGETHER BATMAN AND ROBIN PURSUE HUSH, BATMAN'S CHILDHOOD FRIEND TURNED ENEMY.

PROFILE

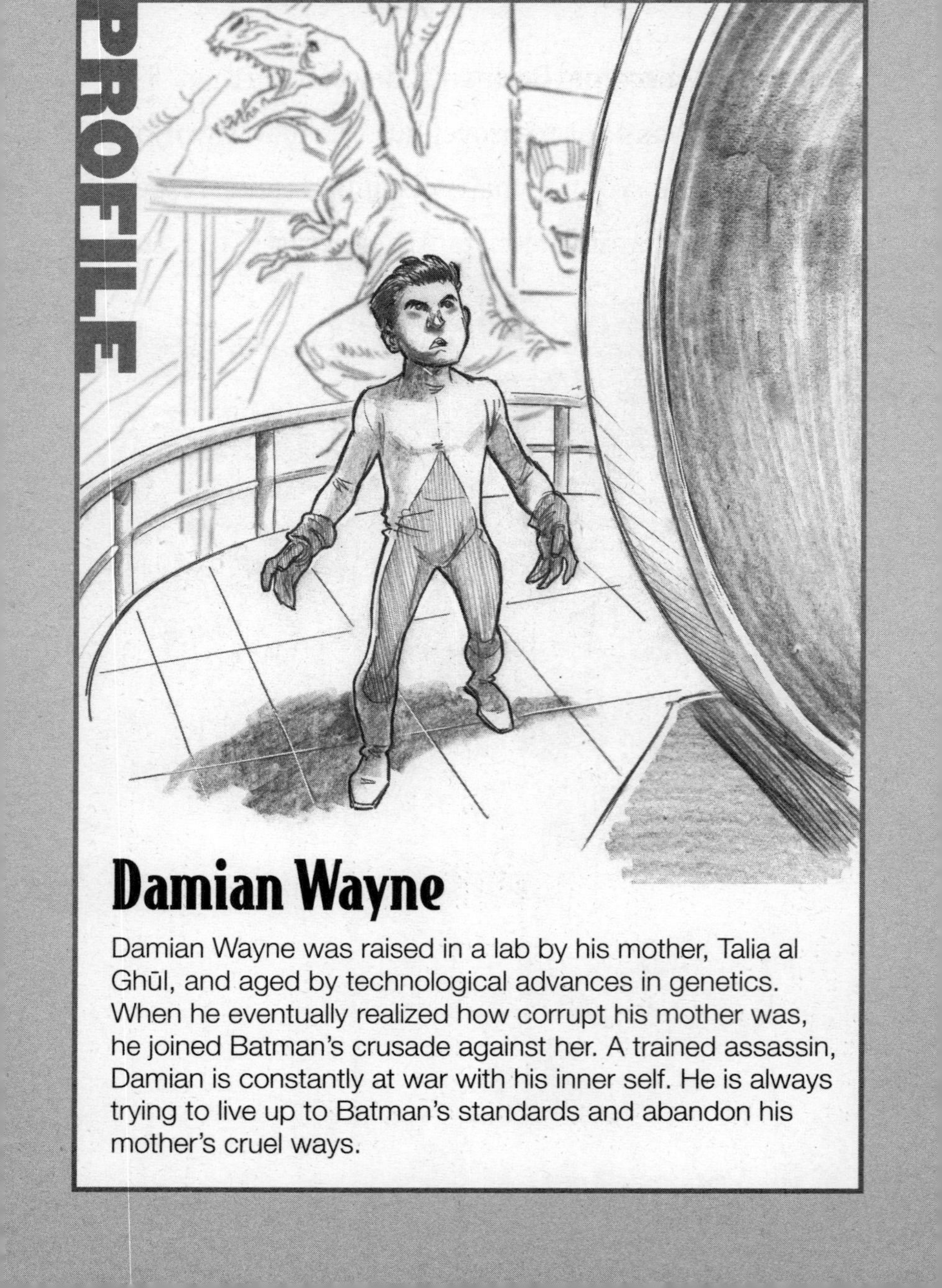

Damian Wayne

Damian Wayne was raised in a lab by his mother, Talia al Ghūl, and aged by technological advances in genetics. When he eventually realized how corrupt his mother was, he joined Batman's crusade against her. A trained assassin, Damian is constantly at war with his inner self. He is always trying to live up to Batman's standards and abandon his mother's cruel ways.

Knight, teaching him just what it means to be a true parent. Batman normally buries his emotions, but where Damian is concerned, he's slowly learning to let his guard down.

The many Robins have done more to help Batman than even the Dark Knight truly realizes. When faced with so much darkness, Batman can often lose sight of his mission. His Robins have given him hope for the future of Gotham City, and brought a little light into his otherwise shadowy world.

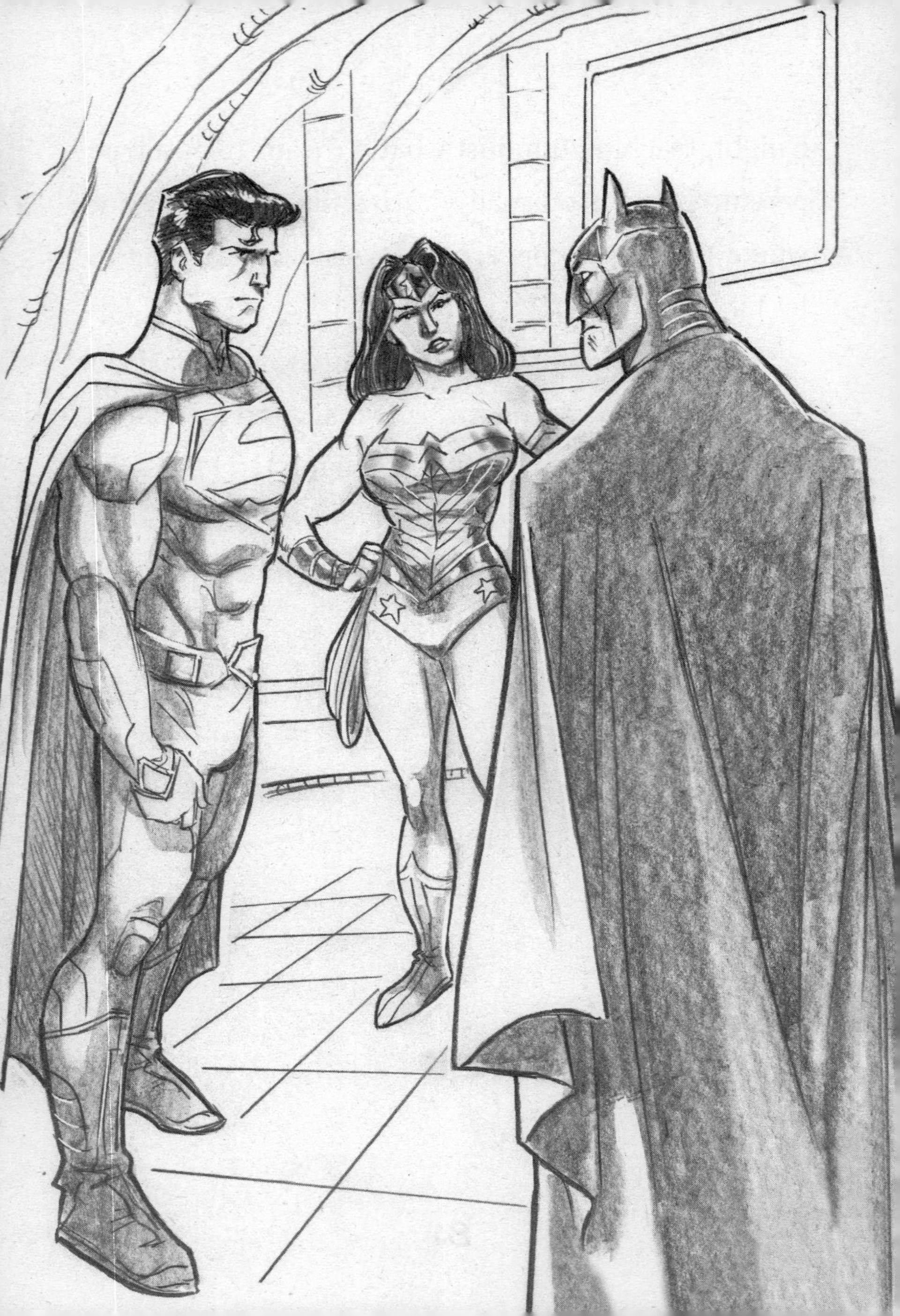

CHAPTER SIX

JUSTICE FOR ALL

Gotham City has enough problems to keep any average crime fighter busy. But there is nothing average about Batman. As he fought to keep Gotham City safe, others were fighting for their own cities all across the country. From alien powerhouse Superman; to amazing Amazon Wonder Woman; to King of the Seven Seas, Aquaman; fantastic heroes were standing up everywhere for the cause of justice. And it didn't take long for these heroes to meet and team up for the greater good.

Batman considered himself a loner rather than a joiner, but when it came to the Justice League, he didn't have much choice. The alien despot Darkseid invaded Earth, and threatened to destroy the entire planet. In order to stop him, Batman found himself partnering with some of the most powerful heroes on the planet. Though teaming with men and women who could bend steel with their bare hands was off-putting at first, Batman realized the good a permanent team of Super Heroes could do for the world. So the Dark

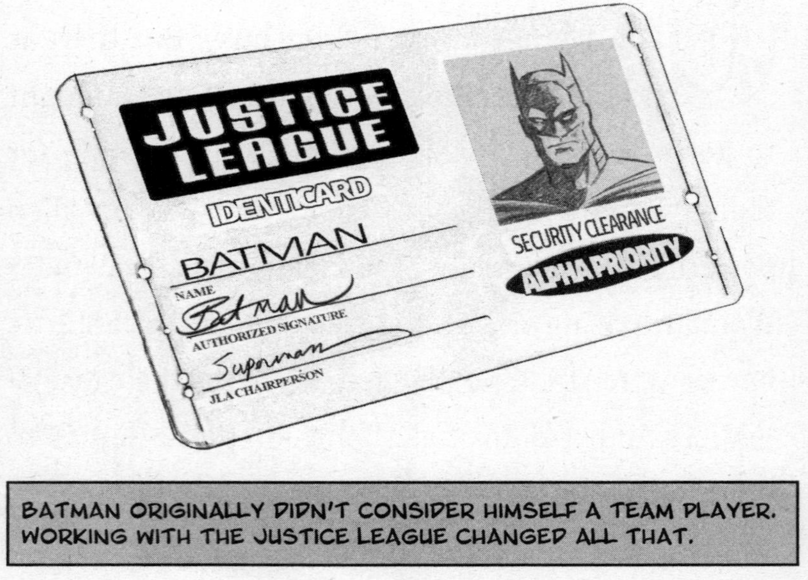
JUSTICE LEAGUE
IDENTICARD
BATMAN
NAME
Batman
AUTHORIZED SIGNATURE
Superman
JLA CHAIRPERSON
SECURITY CLEARANCE
ALPHA PRIORITY

BATMAN ORIGINALLY DIDN'T CONSIDER HIMSELF A TEAM PLAYER. WORKING WITH THE JUSTICE LEAGUE CHANGED ALL THAT.

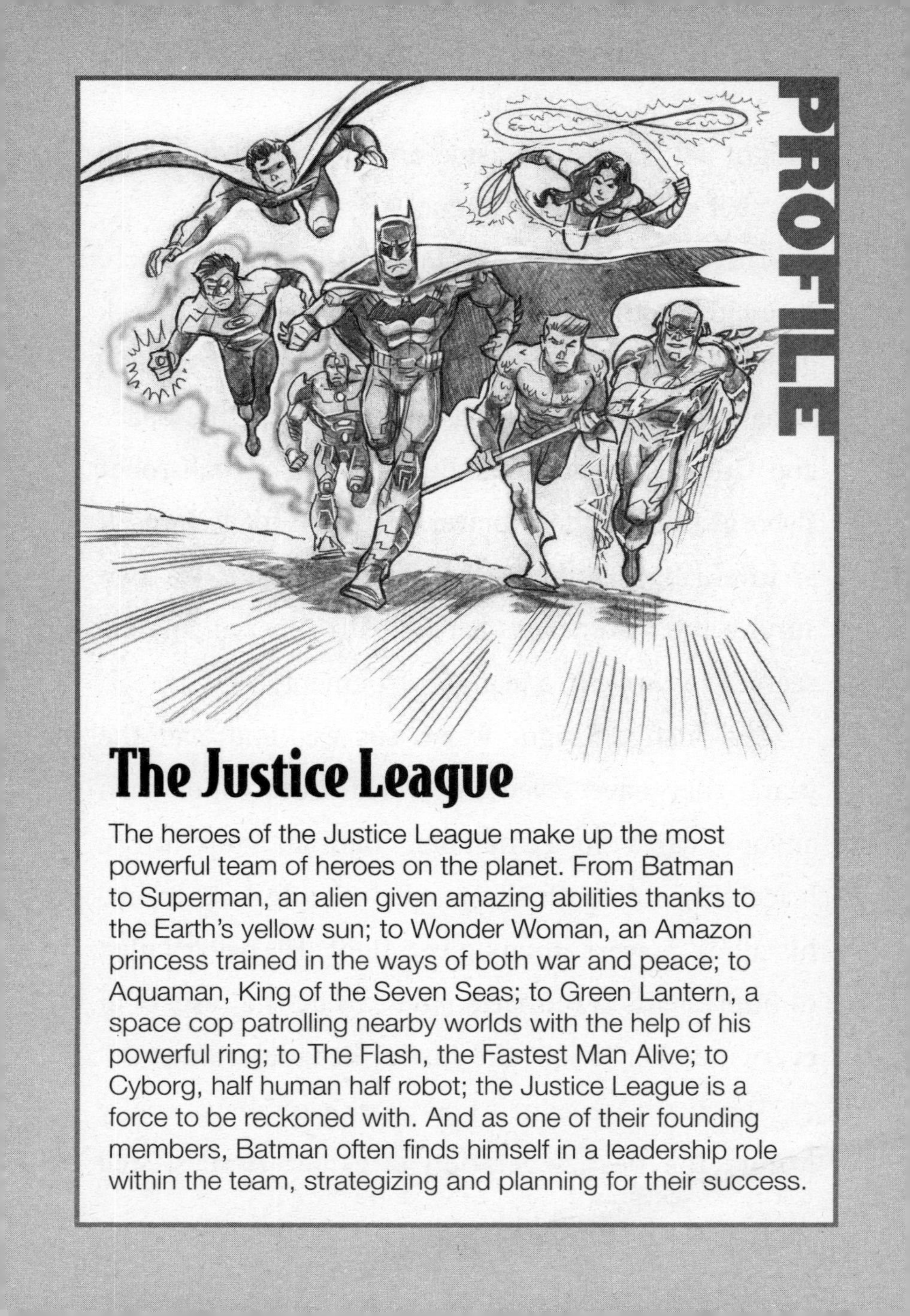

PROFILE

The Justice League

The heroes of the Justice League make up the most powerful team of heroes on the planet. From Batman to Superman, an alien given amazing abilities thanks to the Earth's yellow sun; to Wonder Woman, an Amazon princess trained in the ways of both war and peace; to Aquaman, King of the Seven Seas; to Green Lantern, a space cop patrolling nearby worlds with the help of his powerful ring; to The Flash, the Fastest Man Alive; to Cyborg, half human half robot; the Justice League is a force to be reckoned with. And as one of their founding members, Batman often finds himself in a leadership role within the team, strategizing and planning for their success.

Knight set his doubts aside and became a founding member of the Justice League.

The original Justice League was a diverse bunch. It included the superstrong Superman; the Greek goddess Wonder Woman; the commander of sea life, Aquaman; the super-speedster The Flash; the space cop Green Lantern; and the half-human, half-robot Cyborg. Even without powers, Batman made himself an invaluable member of their team. He did more than survive their numerous battles with supervillains, he seemed to thrive in a team environment.

The Justice League was a success, and over the years, they have saved the world more times than anyone cares to remember. Batman took on a leadership role with the team, learning how to use his allies' powers in any given fight. He never failed to impress his teammates, and earned the respect of every member to join the Justice League's ranks.

The Justice League's teamwork would eventually inspire the next generation of Super Heroes. Red

Robin formed the Teen Titans in the Justice League's image, uniting the young allies of famous heroes, including Wonder Girl, Superboy, and Kid Flash alongside new heroes like Bunker, who can create powerful objects with his mind, and the mysterious Solstice.

THE TEEN TITANS.

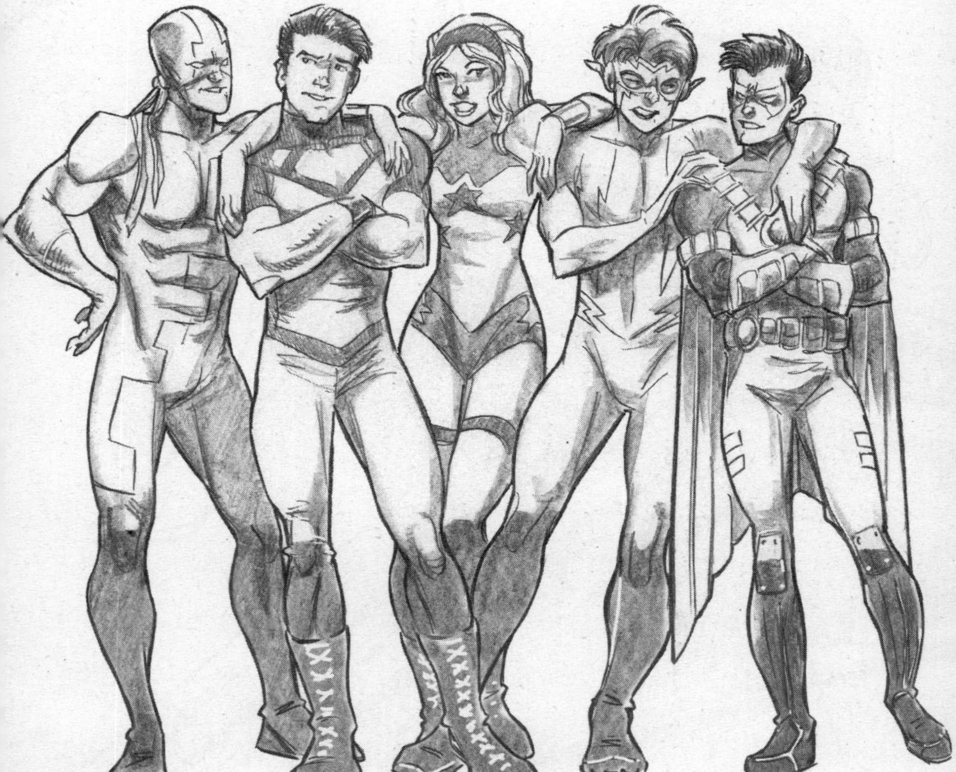

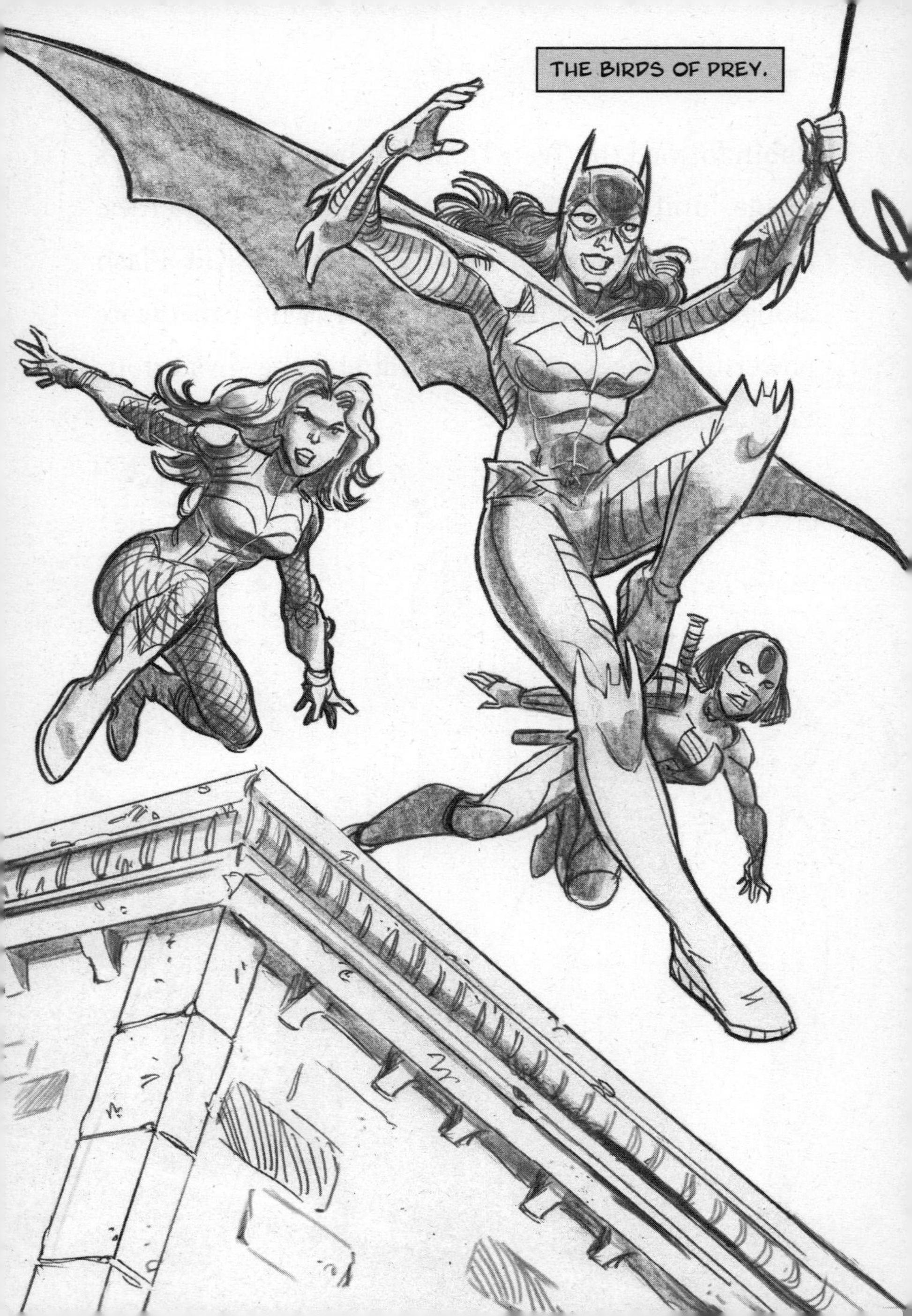
THE BIRDS OF PREY.

A female team of heroes sprouted up as well. Called the Birds of Prey, this team included another of Batman's protégés, Batgirl. She joined forces with heroines including the screeching siren Black Canary and expert martial artist Katana. Alongside the Teen Titans and the Justice League, the Birds of Prey helped to unite the superhuman community even further, keeping Gotham City and the world safe from threats both big and small.

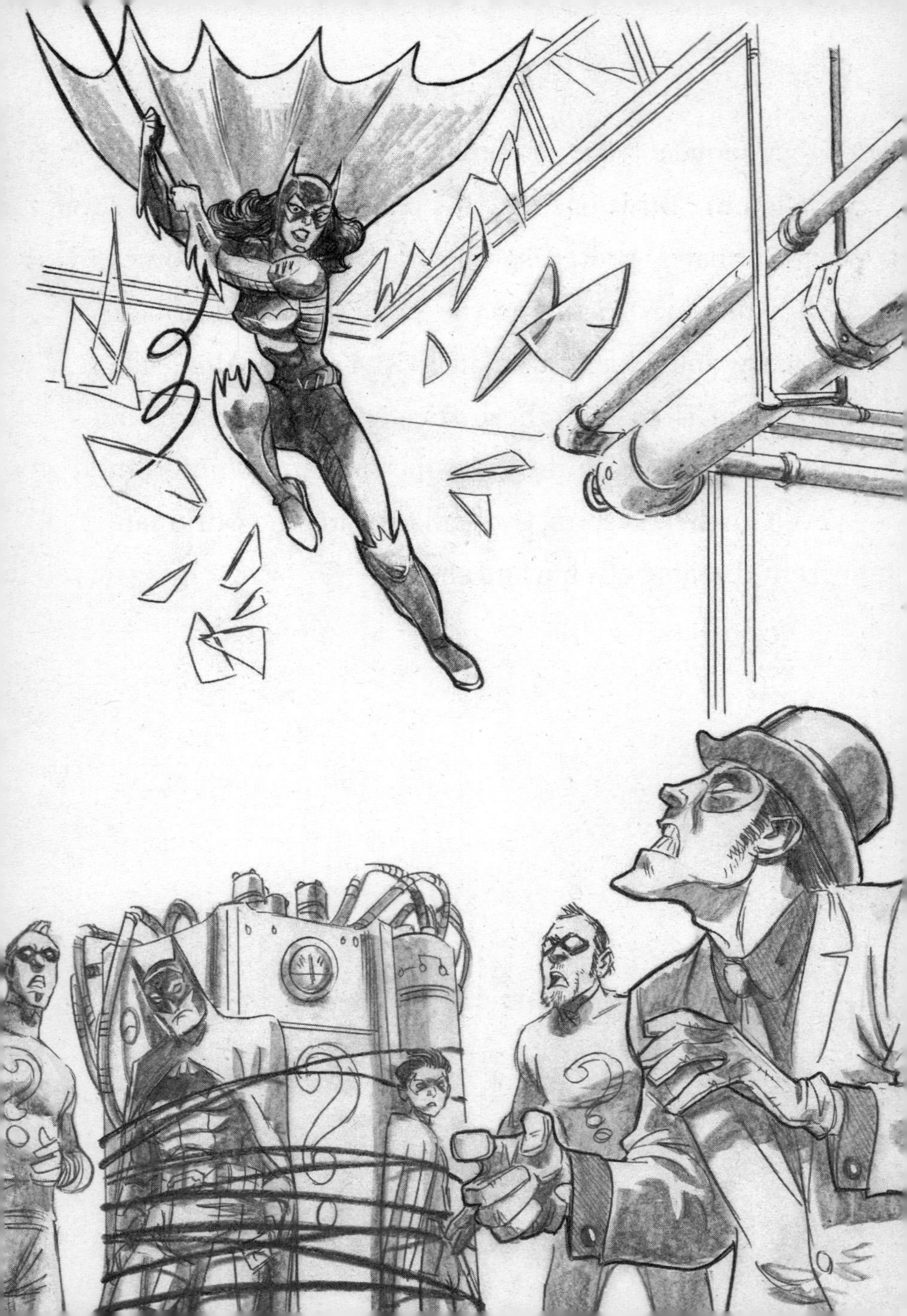

CHAPTER SEVEN

THE ALLIES

The longer Batman continued his crusade on crime, the more men and women became inspired by his example. While there were many people who'd adopt a cape and a cowl because of the actions of the Dynamic Duo, Batgirl was perhaps the greatest success story.

Barbara Gordon is the daughter of Commissioner James Gordon. At an early age, she became interested in martial arts and gymnastics. But more than that, she became interested in protecting Gotham City, like her father and her father's unofficial partner, Batman. While a life in the police force wasn't in the cards for her, she soon took on the role of Batgirl, even though she didn't have Batman's approval.

Batgirl's persistence would eventually impress the Dark Knight. He realized that he couldn't stop her from doing what she wanted to do. His best option was to train her, so she could become the best Batgirl she could be. He took her in as his official partner, and even revealed his dual identity to her. But Batgirl would not be the end of the Batman Family.

COMMISSIONER GORDON DOESN'T KNOW HIS DAUGHTER IS BATGIRL.

PROFILE

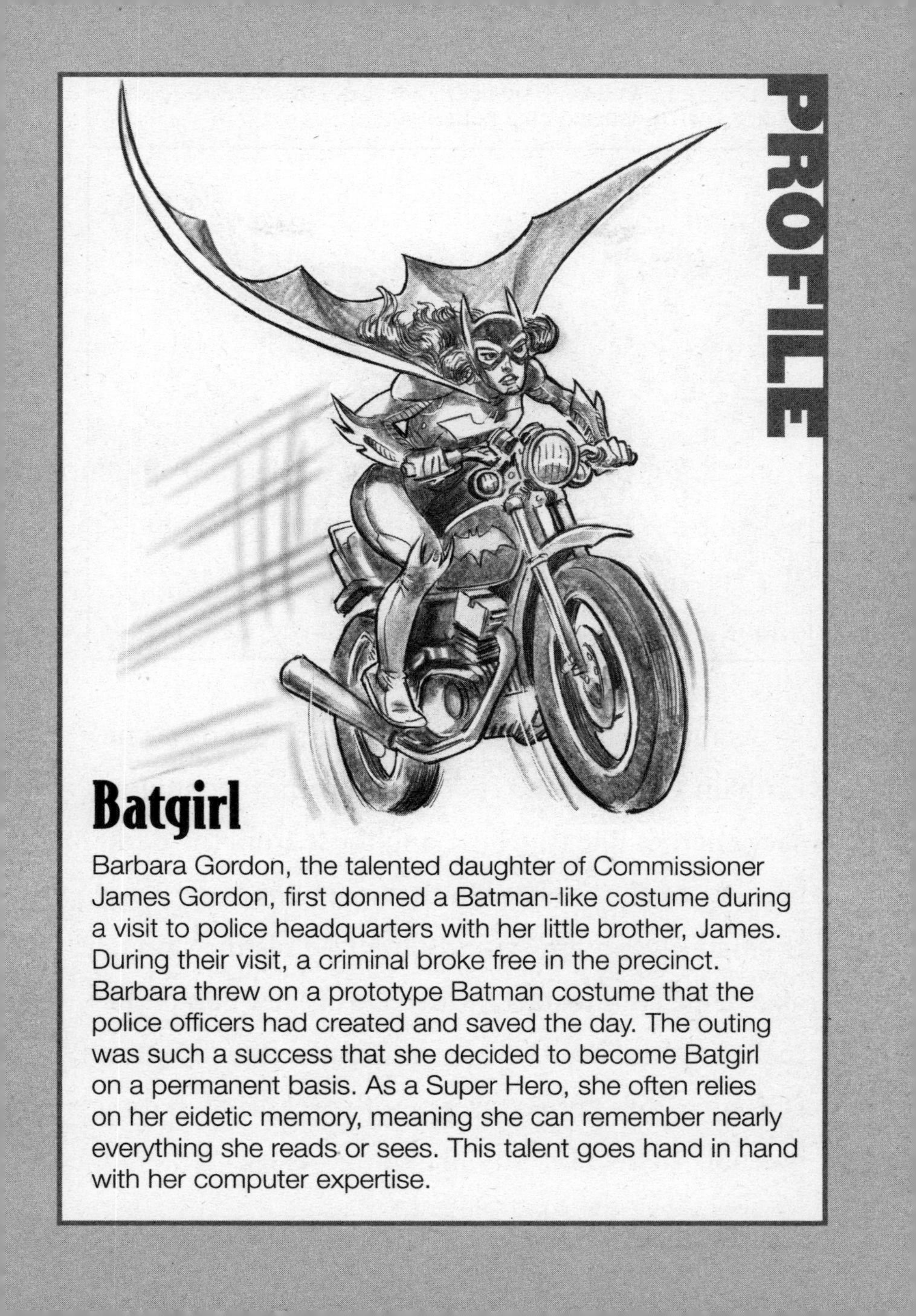

Batgirl

Barbara Gordon, the talented daughter of Commissioner James Gordon, first donned a Batman-like costume during a visit to police headquarters with her little brother, James. During their visit, a criminal broke free in the precinct. Barbara threw on a prototype Batman costume that the police officers had created and saved the day. The outing was such a success that she decided to become Batgirl on a permanent basis. As a Super Hero, she often relies on her eidetic memory, meaning she can remember nearly everything she reads or sees. This talent goes hand in hand with her computer expertise.

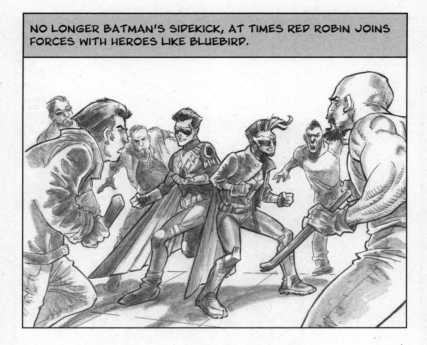

NO LONGER BATMAN'S SIDEKICK, AT TIMES RED ROBIN JOINS FORCES WITH HEROES LIKE BLUEBIRD.

As many Robins came and went, so did other new Gotham City heroes. There were young technology-savvy heroes like Bluebird, and those from the darker corners of the world, like Ragman. In these heroes Batman saw an opportunity to grow his mission. He also helped jump-start the careers of a few new heroes, including the armored crime fighter Batwing. With Gotham City's heroic forces more organized, Batman was able to help his city like never before.

BATMAN IS NOTORIOUSLY TERRITORIAL WHEN IT COMES TO PROTECTING GOTHAM CITY. HEROES LIKE BATWING HAD TO REALLY IMPRESS THE DARK KNIGHT IN ORDER TO WIN HIS TRUST AND EARN A SPOT ON HIS TEAM.

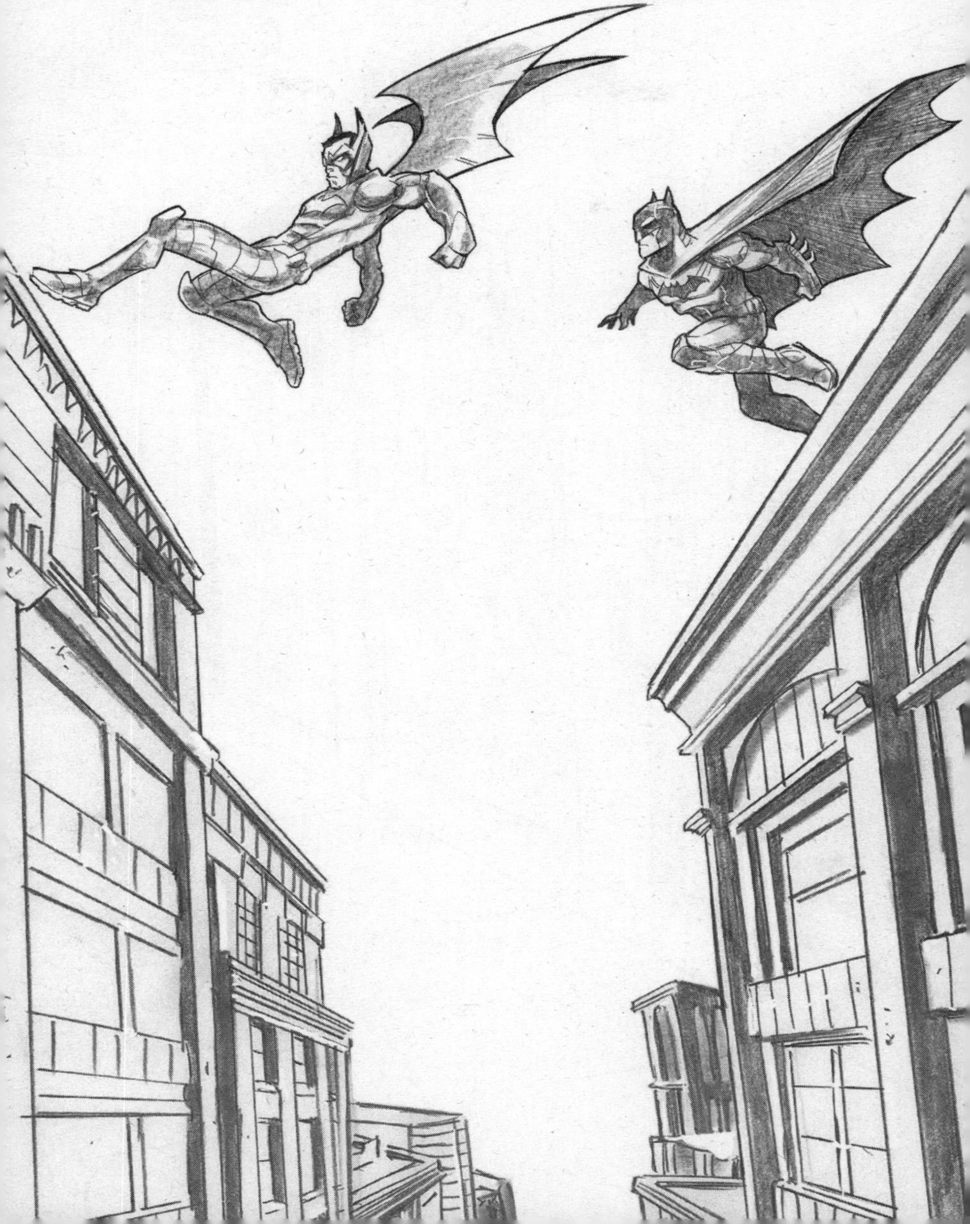

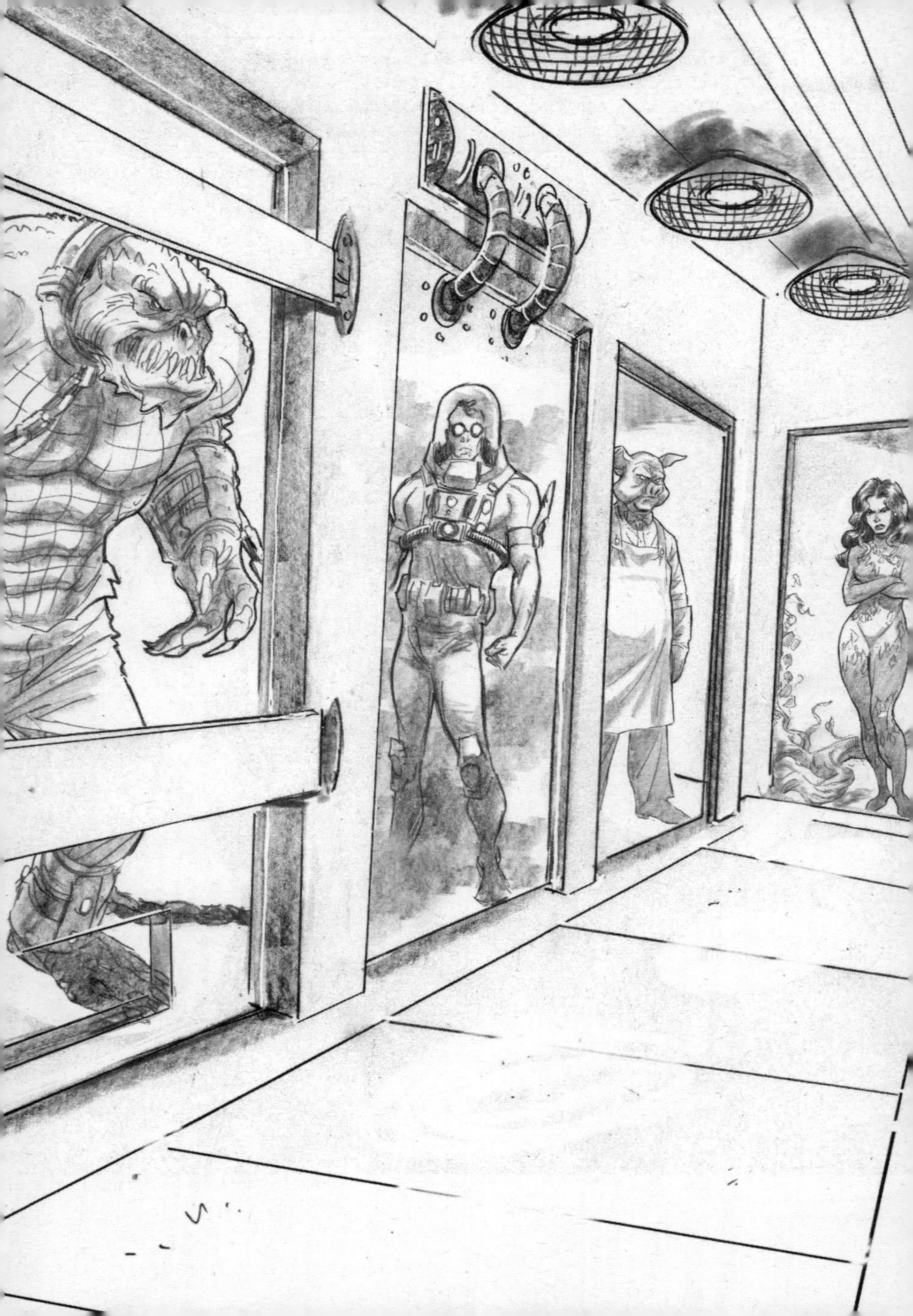

CHAPTER EIGHT

THE ENEMIES

espite Batman's mission to make Gotham City safe, it often seems as if the criminals outnumber the innocents. It is a city overrun by super-villains and madmen. Each presents a unique challenge to the Dark Knight and his allies. Aside from infamous faces like the Joker, the Riddler, and Catwoman, many other bizarre creatures haunted the Gotham City nights at the start of Batman's crusade.

Dr. Hugo Strange was one. He appeared to be a normal psychiatrist to Gotham City's elite, and

INTERVIEW WITH DR. HUGO STRANGE

Any Gothamite who hasn't been living in a cave for the last year has heard of the city's mysterious creature of the night, the so-called Batman. We here at Vue Magazine got the chance to sit down with Professor Hugo Strange, one of the world's leading authorities on this vigilante Caped Crusader, as well as the consultant to Mayor Klass's new vigilante task force.

VUE MAGAZINE: Thanks for taking time out of your busy schedule to talk with us, Dr. Strange.

HUGO STRANGE: It is my pleasure, of course.

VM: Let's talk about how you became associated with the mayor's task force. After all, it's a far cry from your previous work in genetic research.

HS: Ah, yes. Well, as I have learned all too many times, in this day and age, science cannot exist without funding. My foray into genetic engineering was not as well received as I'd hoped by the public at large. It seems Gotham City had other plans for me.

VM: The Batman?

HS: He is a fascinating specimen, isn't he? During the course of my research's fundraising, I actually crossed paths with him. With my psychiatric background, I couldn't help but be intrigued. I had to study him further—to find out what makes him do what he does. My investigation caught the attention of the mayor, and he recruited me for his task force, working alongside the esteemed Captain James Gordon and his second-in-command, Sergeant Max Cort. So now my life has become a journey through the psyche of one of Gotham's most disturbed individuals. Frankly, I find it so interesting, I haven't had time to lament my older scientific endeavors.

VM: And just what are your impressions of Gotham's fabled Dark Knight?

HS: Well, first off, he is very real, not the urban legend some believe him to be. No, he is a man, simple flesh and blood. He can be hurt, and he can be killed. But he's an obsessive man. His ego and sense of self-worth are mind-boggling, really. He possesses an undying thirst for vengeance, yet refuses to go about his quest in a legal, orderly way, say by joining a branch of the local law enforcement, for instance.

VM: You mentioned vengeance. Vengeance for what, exactly?

illustration by Brian Bolland

HS: Most likely some sort of violent crime. It is my firm belief that he watched a family member die before his eyes, probably a spouse, and it changed him. It darkened his worldview and gave birth to a kind of schizophrenia or split personality. He wants glory, but he wants privacy just the same.

VM: There are some out there who would take issue with that point. Captain Gordon, for instance, has stated that he believes the Batman is merely wearing a costume to frighten criminals and to protect his own identity, as many of his alleged actions walk the line between legal and criminal activity.

HS: Captain Gordon is a good man and a good cop, but I'm afraid he lacks an insight to the complexities of the human mind. The Batman wears his costume to feel power, to feel a dark, almost shamanic thrill of the image of a flying, horrible creature. He wants to take back the power that he lost the day he lost his wife.

VM: Thank you for your time, Dr. Strange. You paint a fascinating portrait of the city's most controversial citizen.

HS: And thank you. If you'd like to learn more about what makes the Batman tick, I am currently in the drafting stages of my newest tome, an extended essay on vigilantism and the Batman in particular, entitled *Seduction of the Violent*. If all goes according to schedule, it should be in bookstores by next April.

even a bit of a celebrity. But behind closed doors, Strange was a man obsessed with Batman. Using his knowledge in genetics, he created the Monster Men. These hulking giants were more beast than man. It took all of Batman's ingenuity and the use of many of his signature gadgets to stop the Monster Men. However, Hugo escaped his grasp and continues to be a problem to this day.

Another of Batman's early foes was Clayface. He was originally merely an actor in a mudlike mask named Basil Karlo. However, jealousy over a prized role led to Karlo becoming a murderer. Batman

A SAMPLE OF CLAYFACE'S MORPHING CLAY SUBSTANCE.

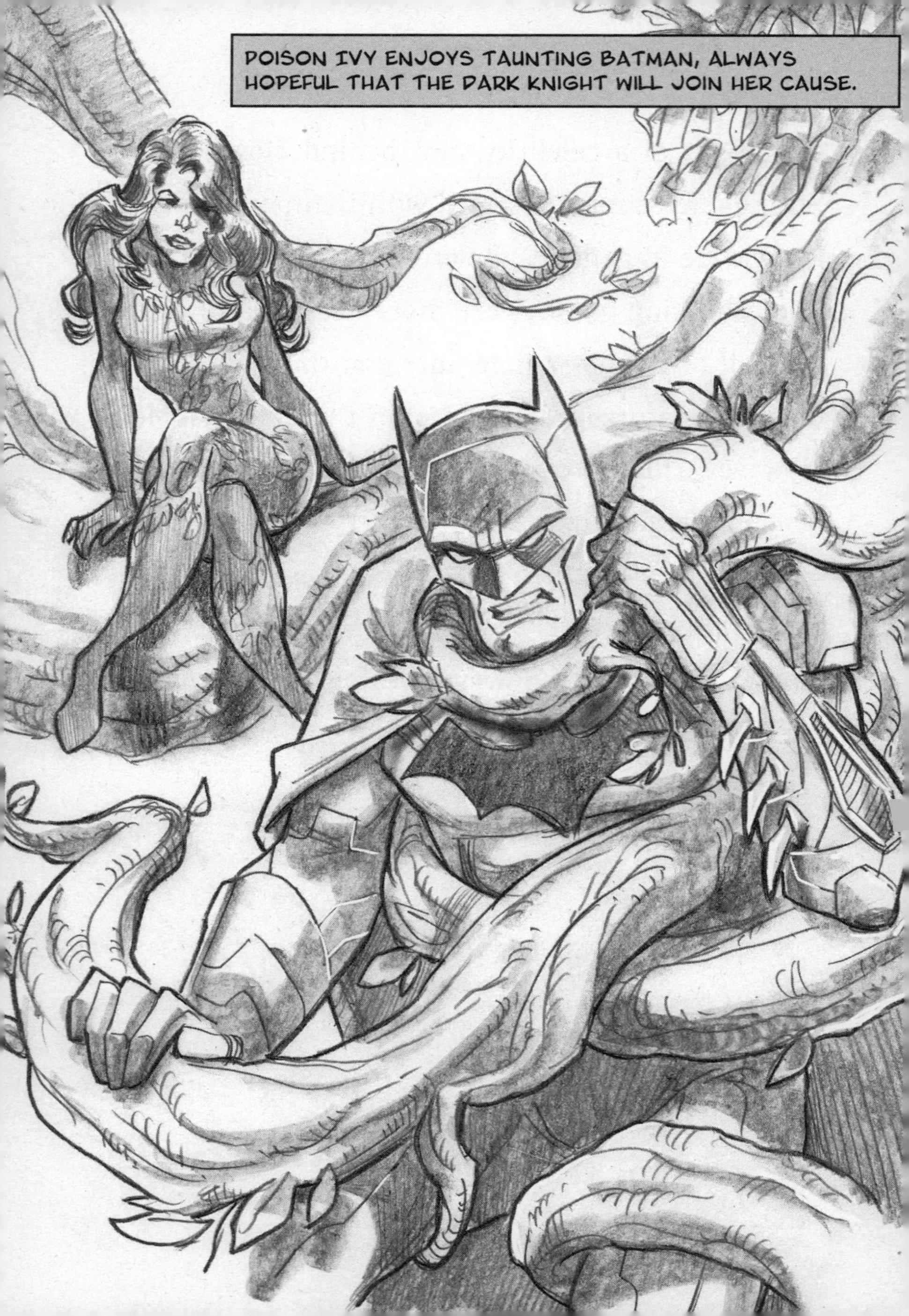
POISON IVY ENJOYS TAUNTING BATMAN, ALWAYS HOPEFUL THAT THE DARK KNIGHT WILL JOIN HER CAUSE.

managed to stop him when they first met, but Clayface would return stronger than the Dark Knight had ever imagined. Karlo injected himself with a formula that transformed his body into a claylike substance. He could shape himself to look like anyone or anything with merely a thought. These days, he has become one of the most powerful and elusive foes in the lineup of villains referred to as Batman's Rogues Gallery.

A constant thorn in Batman's side is Poison Ivy. She is a master of poisons and toxins, and has a natural immunity to her own chemical concoctions. As strange as it seems, Poison Ivy values plant life over human life. She sees the crowded streets of Gotham City as a constant reminder of humankind's domination over the natural world. Poison Ivy would happily exterminate all of mankind for the goal of a greener Earth. Even though Batman values plant life, too, he certainly can't justify her cruel means to an end.

Another face from the early years of Batman's

career, Scarecrow is obsessed with fear in all its forms. He is constantly using Gotham City as his testing grounds for new batches of his fear toxin, a gas that can make anyone see their worst terrors come true before their eyes. Fortunately for Batman, the Dark Knight saw his worst fears years ago and has learned to overcome them, as well as whatever the Scarecrow tries to throw his way.

GOTHAM CITY POLICE
EVIDENCE BAG
INCIDENT:
E110814-1

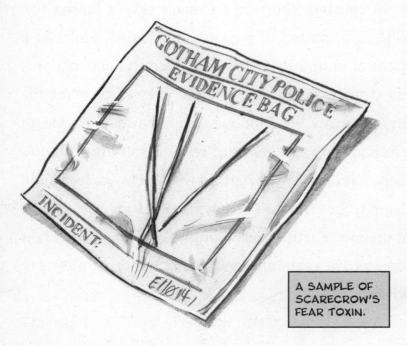

A SAMPLE OF SCARECROW'S FEAR TOXIN.

One of Batman's most powerful enemies, Mr. Freeze mistakenly believes that the Dark Knight contributed to the loss of his wife, Nora. Without her love, Freeze is determined to ensure that the rest of Gotham City shares his pain. He wears a cryogenic

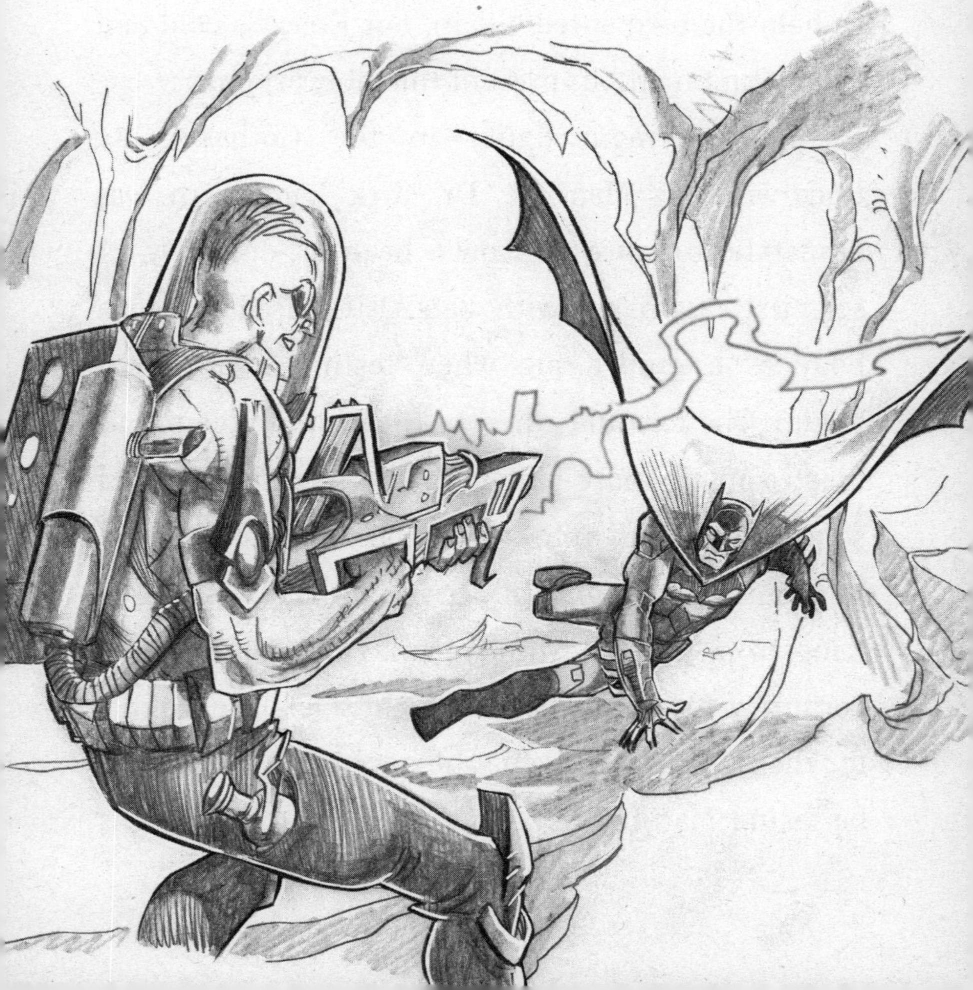

suit that keeps his body at freezing temperatures. He is also armed with a cryo-gun that can instantly freeze anyone in his or her tracks. Mr. Freeze has a cool demeanor, but he makes an exception for Batman. The Dark Knight wants nothing more than to help the tormented villain, but Freeze's cold and calculating methods prevent him at every turn.

Another tragic figure in the Gotham City underworld is Man-Bat. Dr. Kirk Langstrom was desperate to cure his own hearing disability. A scientist fascinated with bats, Kirk used his own body as a guinea pig when testing a bat-based serum. The formula cured his hearing problem, but created many more issues for the scientist. He was soon transformed into a giant hulking bat creature rampaging through the city. Batman has cured Langstrom time and time again. However, Man-Bat continues to reemerge in the night skies. The trouble for the Dark Knight is that he never knows if he will be facing Man-Bat as a friend or a foe. Man-Bat is

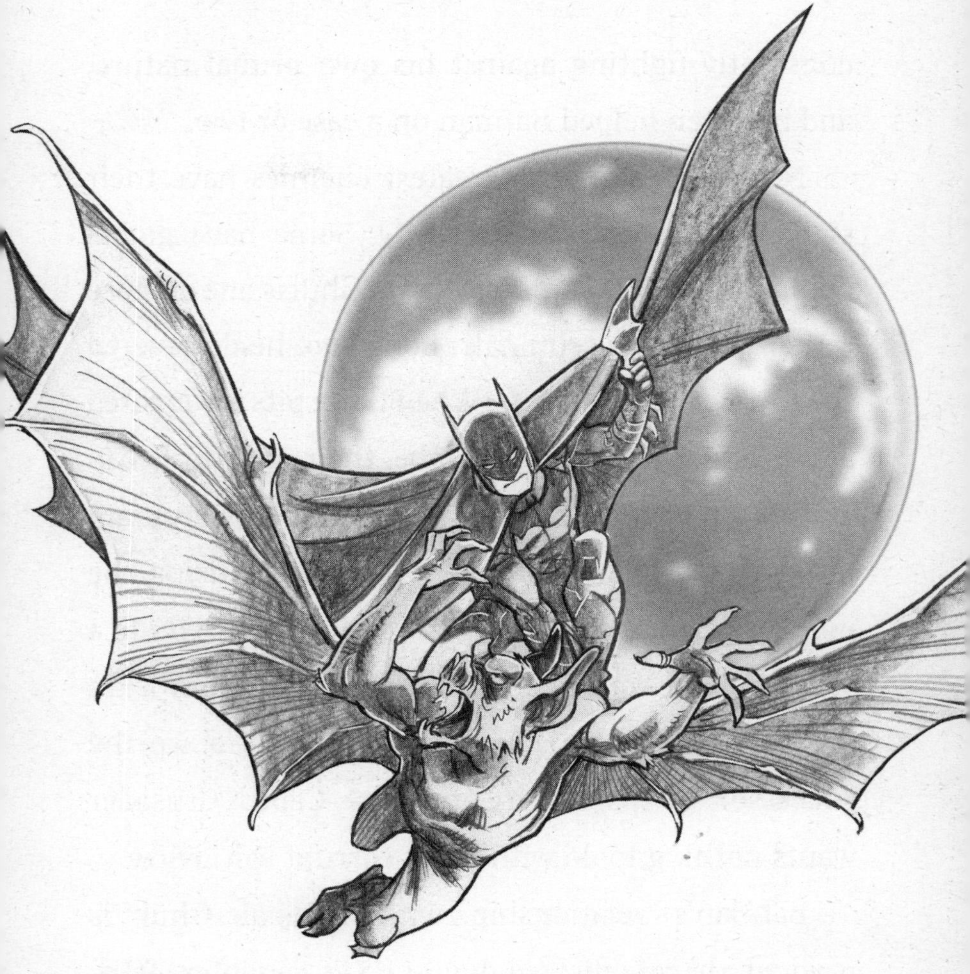

SOMETIMES BATMAN AND MAN-BAT ARE ALLIES, BUT, MORE OFTEN THAN NOT, THEY ARE ENEMIES.

constantly fighting against his own primal nature, and has even helped Batman on a case or two.

Not all of Batman's greatest enemies have their sights set on just Gotham City. Some have global domination on their minds. Rā's al Ghūl is one of those rather ambitious criminals. Long ago, he discovered the mystical Lazarus Pits. When these pits are created at particular spots on the globe, their chemicals can restore a person's health, like the legendary fountain of youth. Rā's has survived for centuries using the pits' properties. This has allowed him time to build a vast criminal empire and become one of the world's greatest terrorists. He views Batman as a worthy successor to his empire, but the Caped Crusader wants nothing to do with Rā's's corrupt worldview.

Batman's relationship with Rā's al Ghūl is particularly complicated due to Rā's's daughter, Talia. Batman and Talia have long had feelings for each other. They have had an on-again, off-again relationship for many years. In fact, Talia and Batman even have a

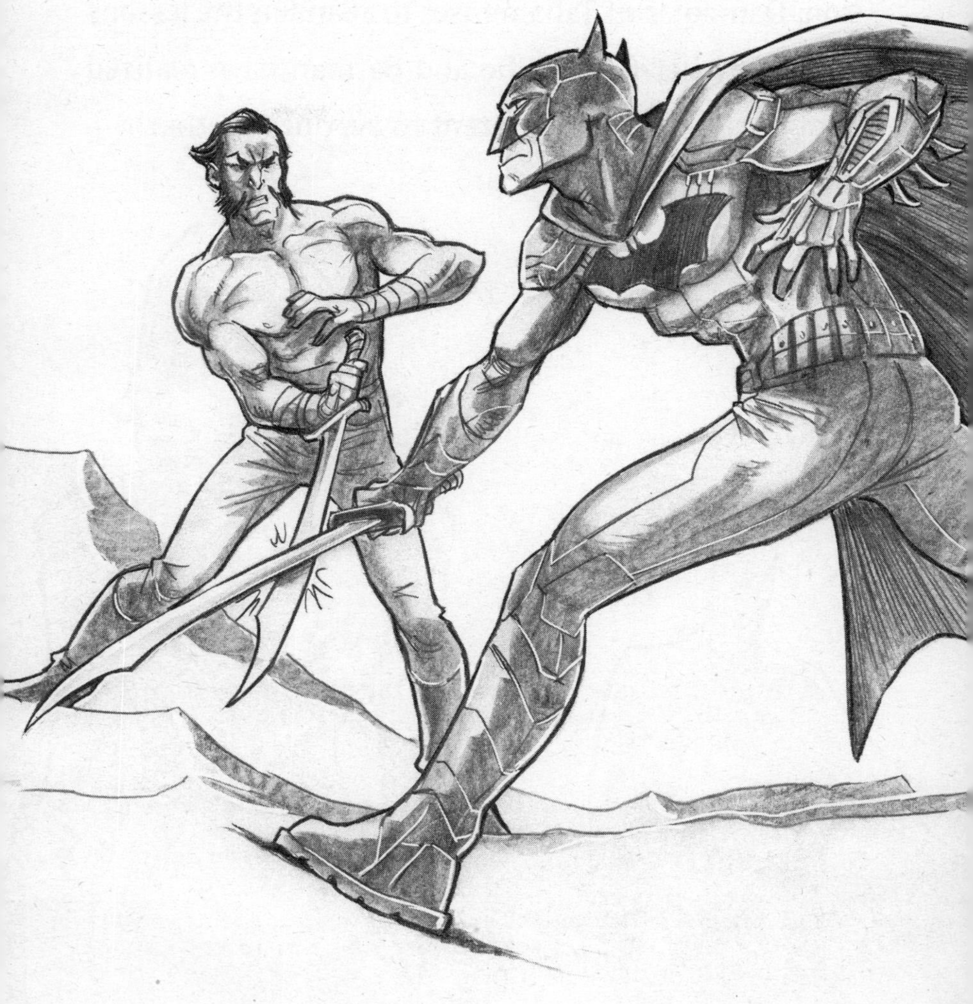

THE NEAR-IMMORTAL RĀ'S AL GHŪL IS ONE OF BATMAN'S DEADLIEST FOES, AND THE GRANDFATHER OF HIS ONLY SON, DAMIAN.

son, Damian. But Talia refuses to abandon the lessons taught by her father. She and Batman have realized that they are far too different to ever be together.

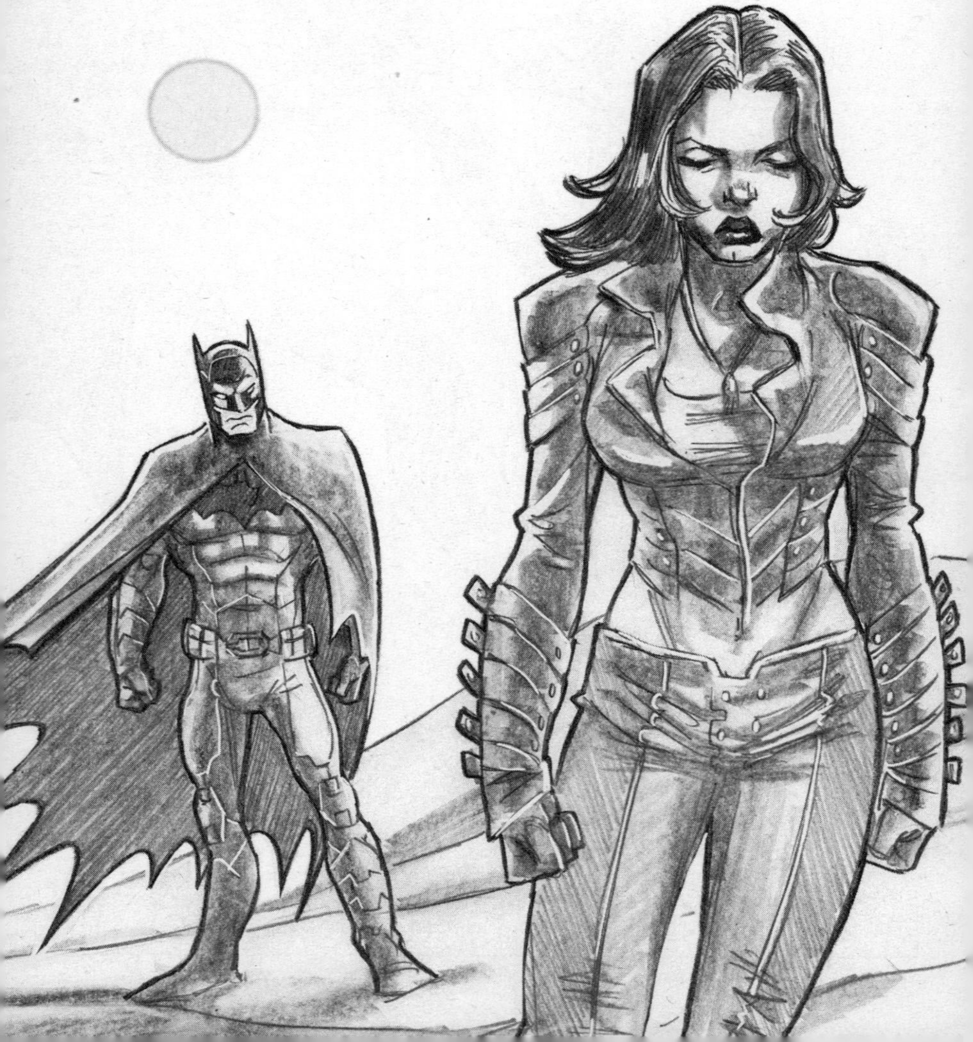

PROFILE

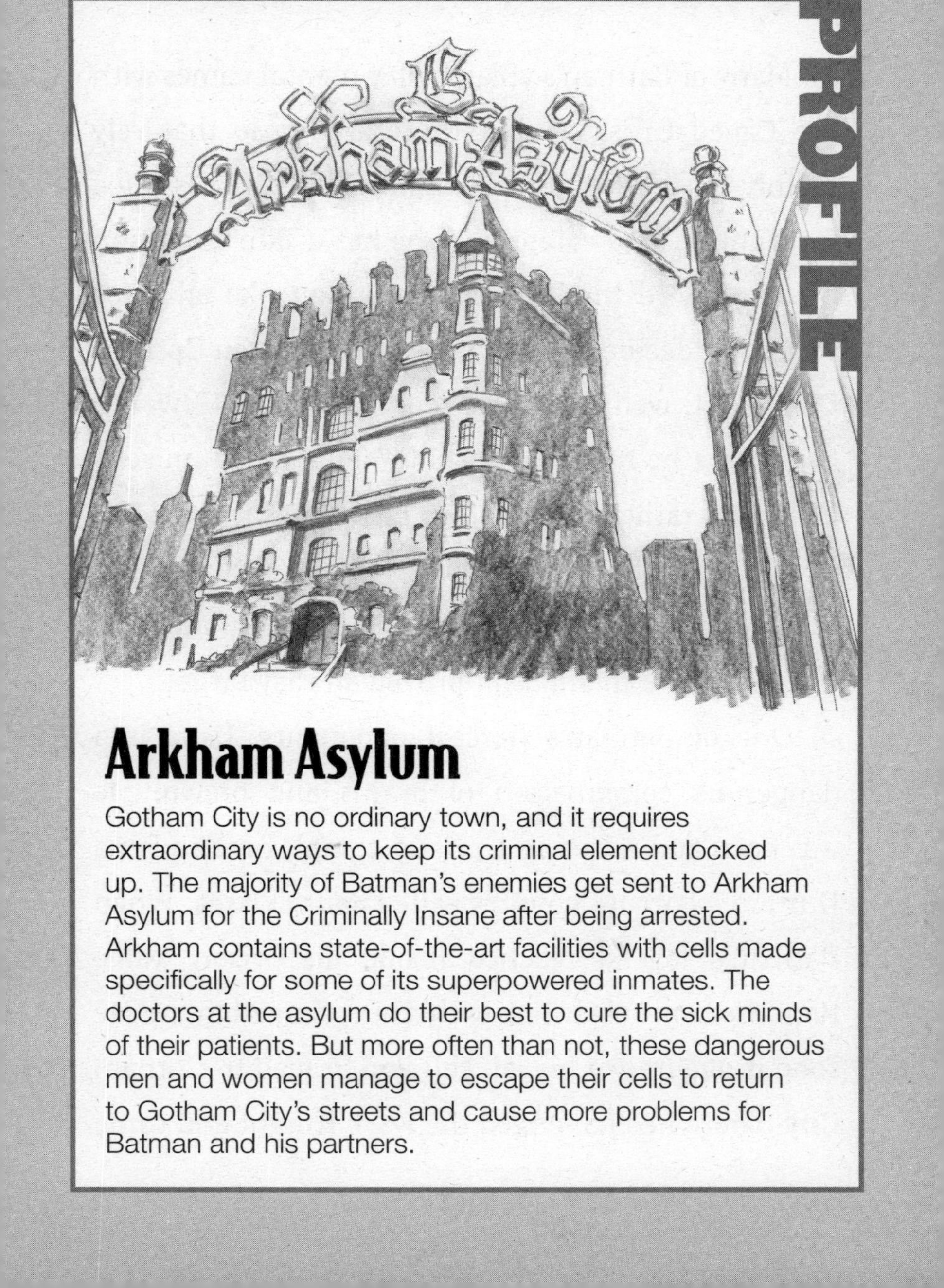
Arkham Asylum

Arkham Asylum

Gotham City is no ordinary town, and it requires extraordinary ways to keep its criminal element locked up. The majority of Batman's enemies get sent to Arkham Asylum for the Criminally Insane after being arrested. Arkham contains state-of-the-art facilities with cells made specifically for some of its superpowered inmates. The doctors at the asylum do their best to cure the sick minds of their patients. But more often than not, these dangerous men and women manage to escape their cells to return to Gotham City's streets and cause more problems for Batman and his partners.

Many of Batman's villains play mental games with the Caped Crusader, but there are those that rely mainly on their physical might. Killer Croc is a foe from the second category. Croc has a skin condition that hardened his flesh to something like alligator scales. He decided to become a crime boss in Gotham City after traveling with a circus freak show. However, these days he mostly resorts to being hired muscle. He would rather not plan out his crimes if given the choice. For Killer Croc, life is easier when he only has to worry about hitting something. Unfortunately for the villain, Batman hasn't proved an easy target.

One of Batman's fiercest opponents, Bane is a dangerous combination of brains and brawn. He was born and raised in a prison complex called Peña Duro in a corrupt country called Santa Prisca. When Batman's legend reached inside his prison walls, Bane became obsessed with the crime fighter. He soon broke free of his jail cell and headed to Gotham City. There he challenged the Dark Knight and came

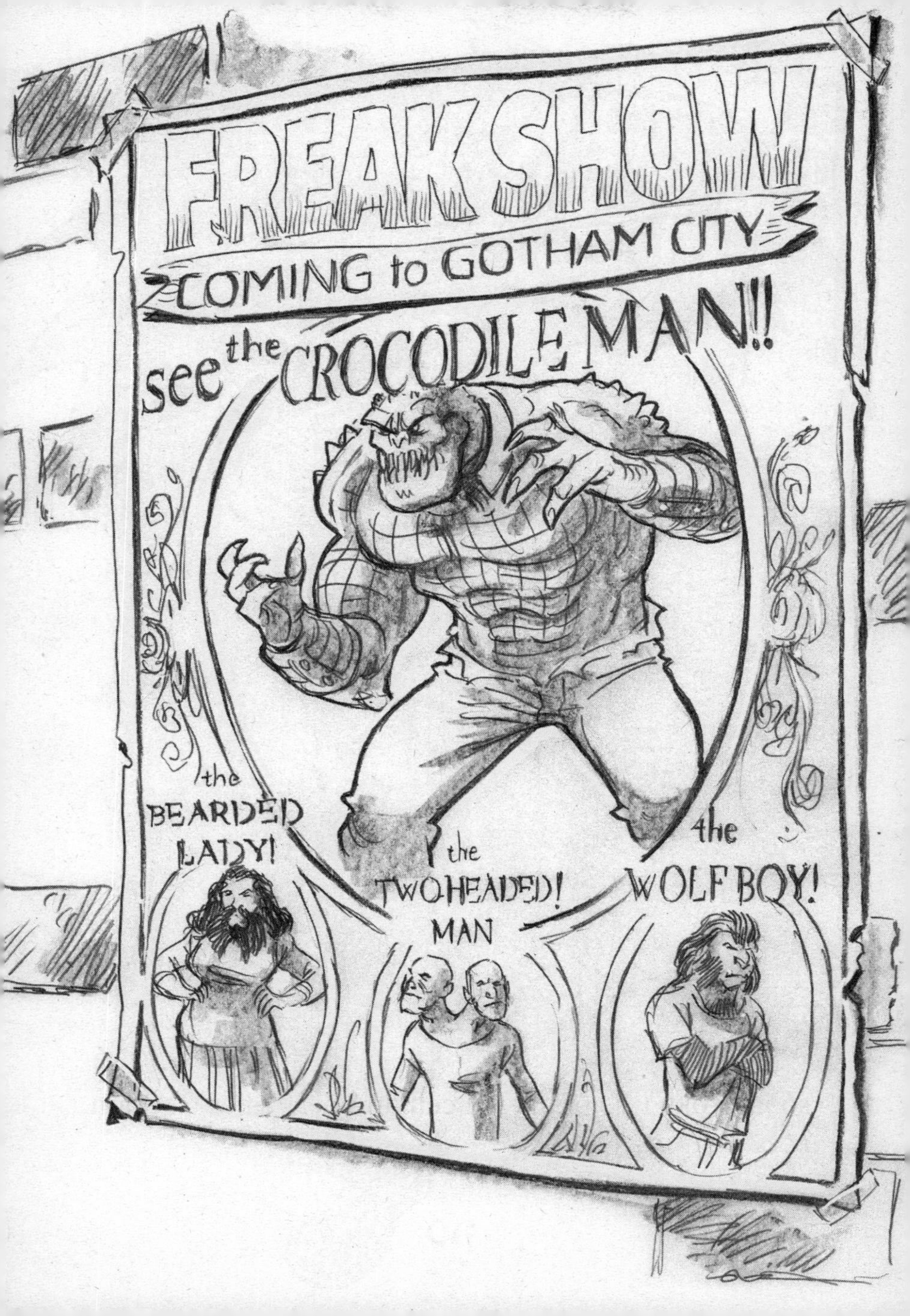
FREAK SHOW
COMING to GOTHAM CITY
see the CROCODILE MAN!!
the BEARDED LADY!
the TWO-HEADED! MAN
the WOLF BOY!

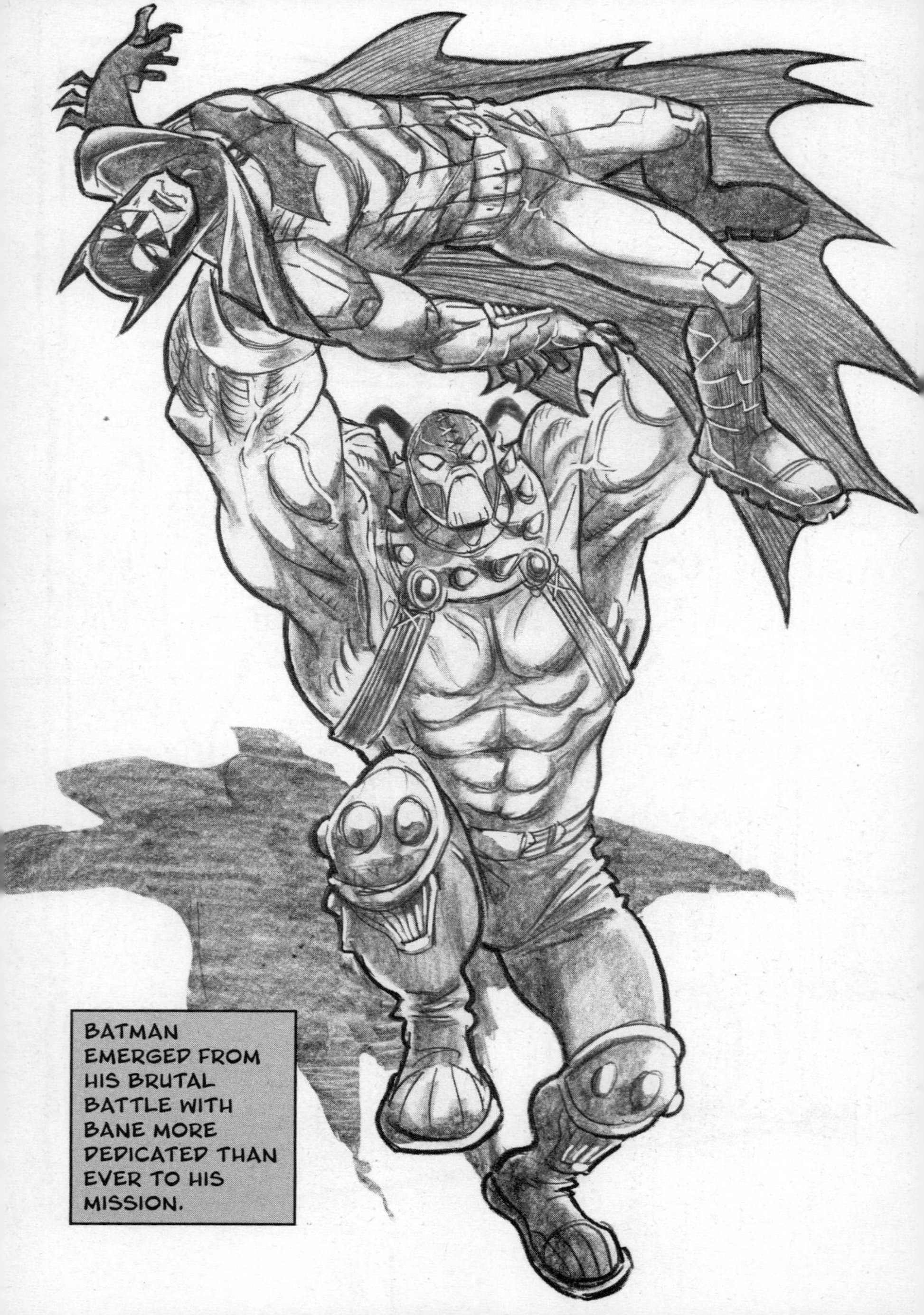
BATMAN EMERGED FROM HIS BRUTAL BATTLE WITH BANE MORE DEDICATED THAN EVER TO HIS MISSION.

closer to breaking Batman than any villain before him. However, Bruce Wayne soon trained his body back to its near-perfect state. Batman confronted Bane in a rematch that saw the villain jailed once more.

Batman has also had to contend with innocents being tainted and influenced by the many notable criminals lurking in Gotham City. One such impressionable person was Dr. Harleen Quinzel, a psychiatrist at Arkham Asylum who fell madly in love with the Joker. She soon adopted her own

DR. HARLEEN QUINZEL WENT FROM DOCTOR TO DELINQUENT AFTER TREATING THE JOKER.

clown costume and became the villain Harley Quinn. Harley has tried ever since to warm the Joker's cold, cruel heart. Despite Batman's best intentions to help her, Harley has been unable to shake her feelings for Gotham City's famed Clown Prince of Crime.

As if those dangerous threats weren't enough to keep Batman and his allies busy, there have been many more criminals to darken Gotham City's streets over the years. The mind-controlling Mad Hatter is obsessed with both hats and Lewis Carroll's Alice in

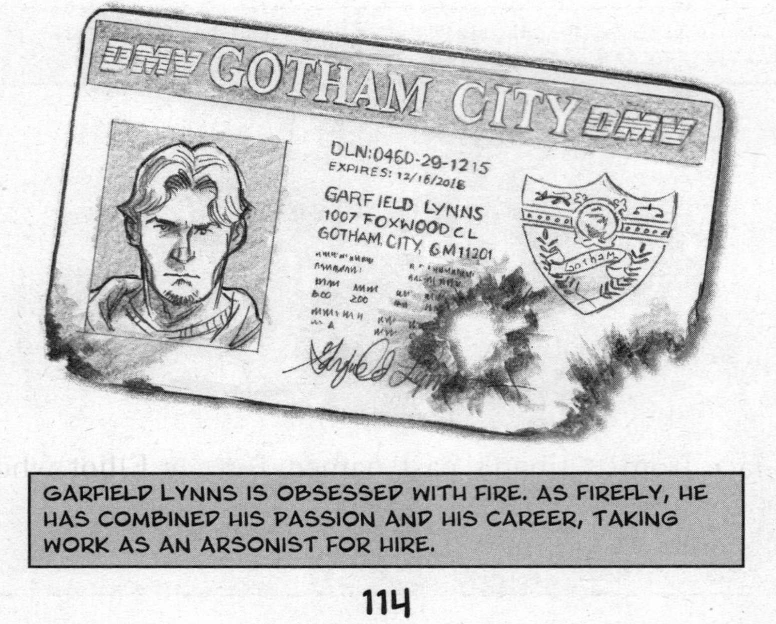
DMV GOTHAM CITY DMV
DLN:0460-29-1215
EXPIRES: 12/16/2018
GARFIELD LYNNS
1007 FOXWOOD CL
GOTHAM CITY, GM11201
Gotham

GARFIELD LYNNS IS OBSESSED WITH FIRE. AS FIREFLY, HE HAS COMBINED HIS PASSION AND HIS CAREER, TAKING WORK AS AN ARSONIST FOR HIRE.

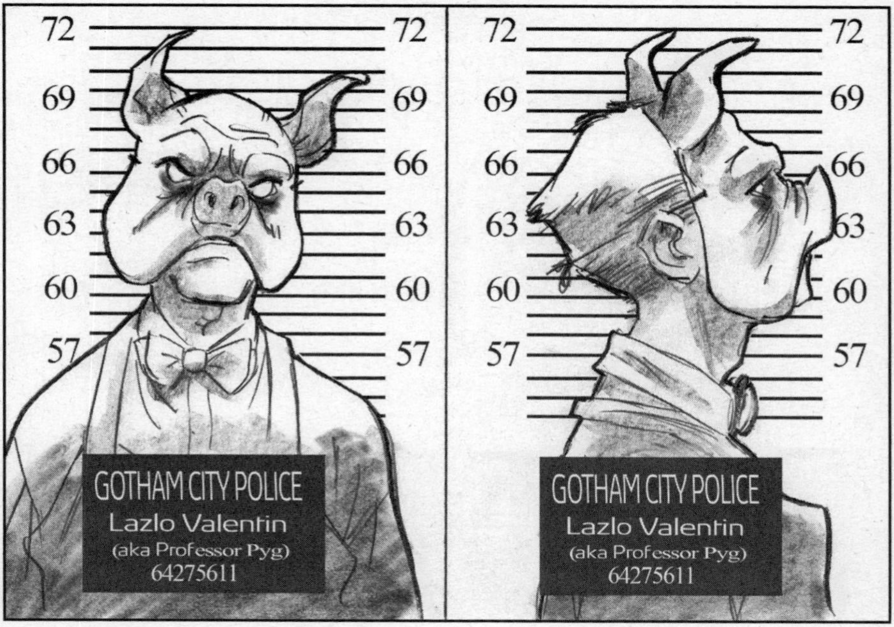
72
69
66
63
60
57
GOTHAM CITY POLICE
Lazlo Valentin
(aka Professor Pyg)
64275611
GOTHAM CITY POLICE
Lazlo Valentin
(aka Professor Pyg)
64275611

PROFESSOR PYG BECAME A MAJOR NEW THREAT TO THE BATMAN IN RECENT MONTHS. HE HAS A TWISTED MIND, AND EMPLOYS A SMALL ARMY OF HENCHMEN THAT HE CALLS DOLLOTRONS.

Wonderland stories. Firefly is a dangerous arsonist who simply wants to watch Gotham City burn. Black Mask is a crime lord with a beef against both Bruce Wayne and Batman. The Ventriloquist uses a dummy to commit heinous criminal acts. Hush is a face from Batman's past named Tommy Elliot who discovered Bruce Wayne's every secret in order to use

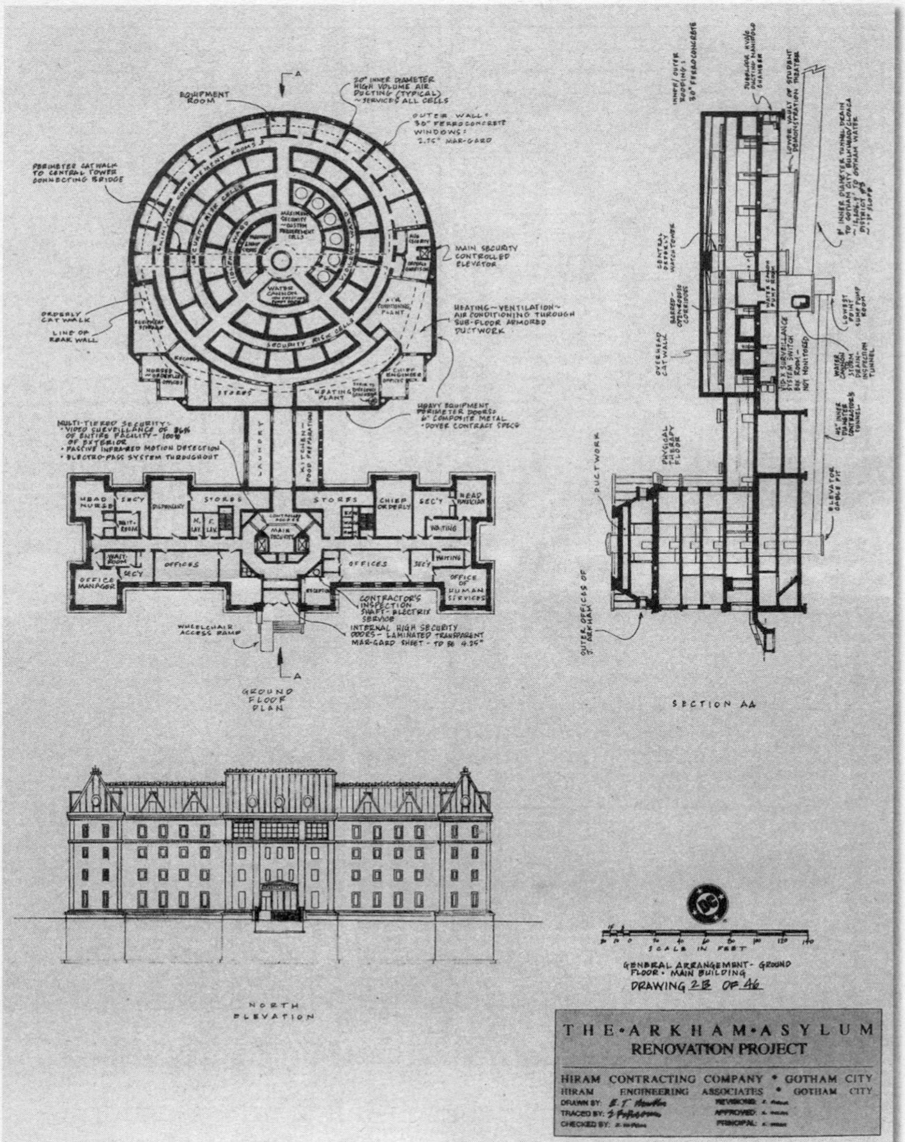
EQUIPMENT ROOM
20" INNER DIAMETER HIGH VOLUME AIR DUCTING (TYPICAL) ~SERVICES ALL CELLS
OUTER WALL: 30" FERROCONCRETE WINDOWS: 2.75" MAR-GARD
PERIMETER CATWALK TO CENTRAL TOWER CONNECTING BRIDGE
MAIN SECURITY CONTROLLED ELEVATOR
ORDERLY CATWALK
LINE OF REAR WALL
HEATING~VENTILATION~AIR CONDITIONING THROUGH SUB-FLOOR ARMORED DUCTWORK
HEAVY EQUIPMENT PERIMETER DOORS: 6" COMPOSITE METAL ·DOVER CONTRACT SPECS
MULTI-TIERED SECURITY: ·VIDEO SURVEILLANCE OF 86% OF ENTIRE FACILITY · 100% OF EXTERIOR ·PASSIVE INFRARED MOTION DETECTION ·ELECTRO-PASS SYSTEM THROUGHOUT
STORES
OFFICES
CHIEF ORDERLY
SEC'Y
WAITING
OFFICE MANAGER
OFFICE OF HUMAN SERVICES
CONTRACTOR'S INSPECTION SHAFT-ELECTRIX SERVICE
INTERNAL HIGH SECURITY DOORS - LAMINATED TRANSPARENT MAR-GARD SHEET - TO BE 4.25"
WHEELCHAIR ACCESS RAMP
GROUND FLOOR PLAN
SECTION AA
DUCTWORK
OUTER OFFICES OF ARKHAM
NORTH ELEVATION
SCALE IN FEET
GENERAL ARRANGEMENT - GROUND FLOOR · MAIN BUILDING
DRAWING 2B OF 46
THE·ARKHAM·ASYLUM
RENOVATION PROJECT
HIRAM CONTRACTING COMPANY · GOTHAM CITY
HIRAM ENGINEERING ASSOCIATES · GOTHAM CITY
DRAWN BY:
TRACED BY:
CHECKED BY:
REVISIONS:
APPROVED:
PRINCIPAL:

BATMAN KEEPS ARKHAM ASYLUM FULL WITH HIS MANY FOES.

them against him. Professor Pyg is a recent addition to Batman's Rogues Gallery. He considers himself an "artist," and is not above committing murder to make his artistic statement.

The list of the members of Batman's Rogues Gallery goes on and on. In fact, the Dark Knight finds it difficult to keep up with all his villains, even with the aid of his sophisticated Batcomputer. There are many horrors that continue to go bump in the Gotham City night. Luckily for its citizens, Batman remains the most terrifying one.

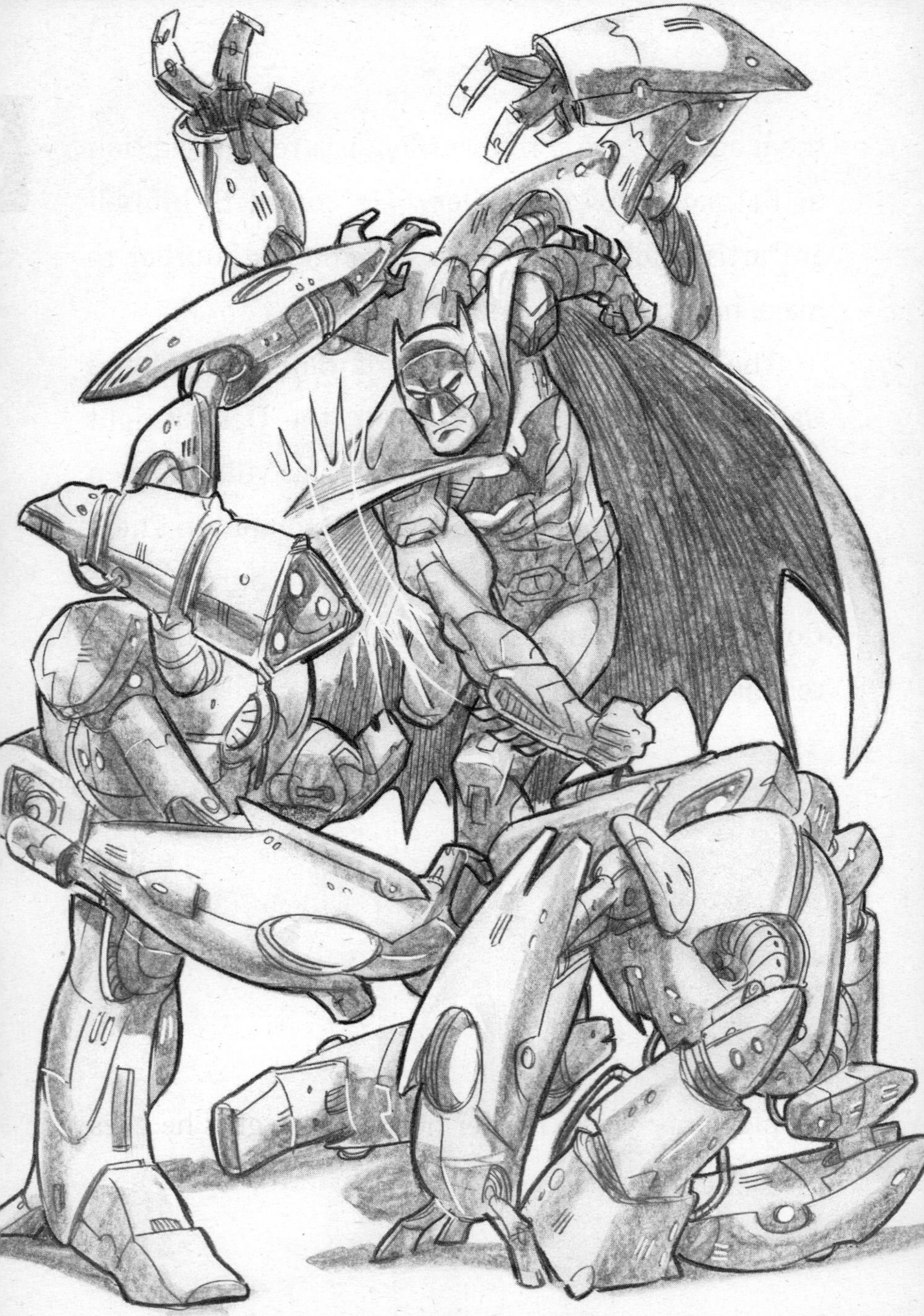

CHAPTER NINE

THE FUTURE

Over the years, Batman has learned that one man can indeed make a difference. He has truly changed Gotham City for the better. The streets are a little safer. The police force is a little less corrupt. Yet there is still a need for a Batman. And that need doesn't seem to be going away anytime soon. If there is one thing Batman has learned during his career, it is that Gotham City has a constant supply of crime. No matter how many nights he goes on patrol, or how many allies aid him in his quest, there seems to be a wealth of men and women willing to take the easy way out and break the law.

But as long as he is able, Bruce Wayne will continue his crusade. He will not—and perhaps cannot—give up on his city or his mission. Only time will tell if the role of Batman will one day be passed on to one of his longtime partners, or if someone new will decide to don the mantle of the bat. But it seems no matter the man behind the mask, there will always be a Batman. The Dark Knight will be around until the impossible day that Gotham City is free from crime. Only then will there be no need for Batman. And only then will a little boy's promise made on the graves of his parents finally be fulfilled.

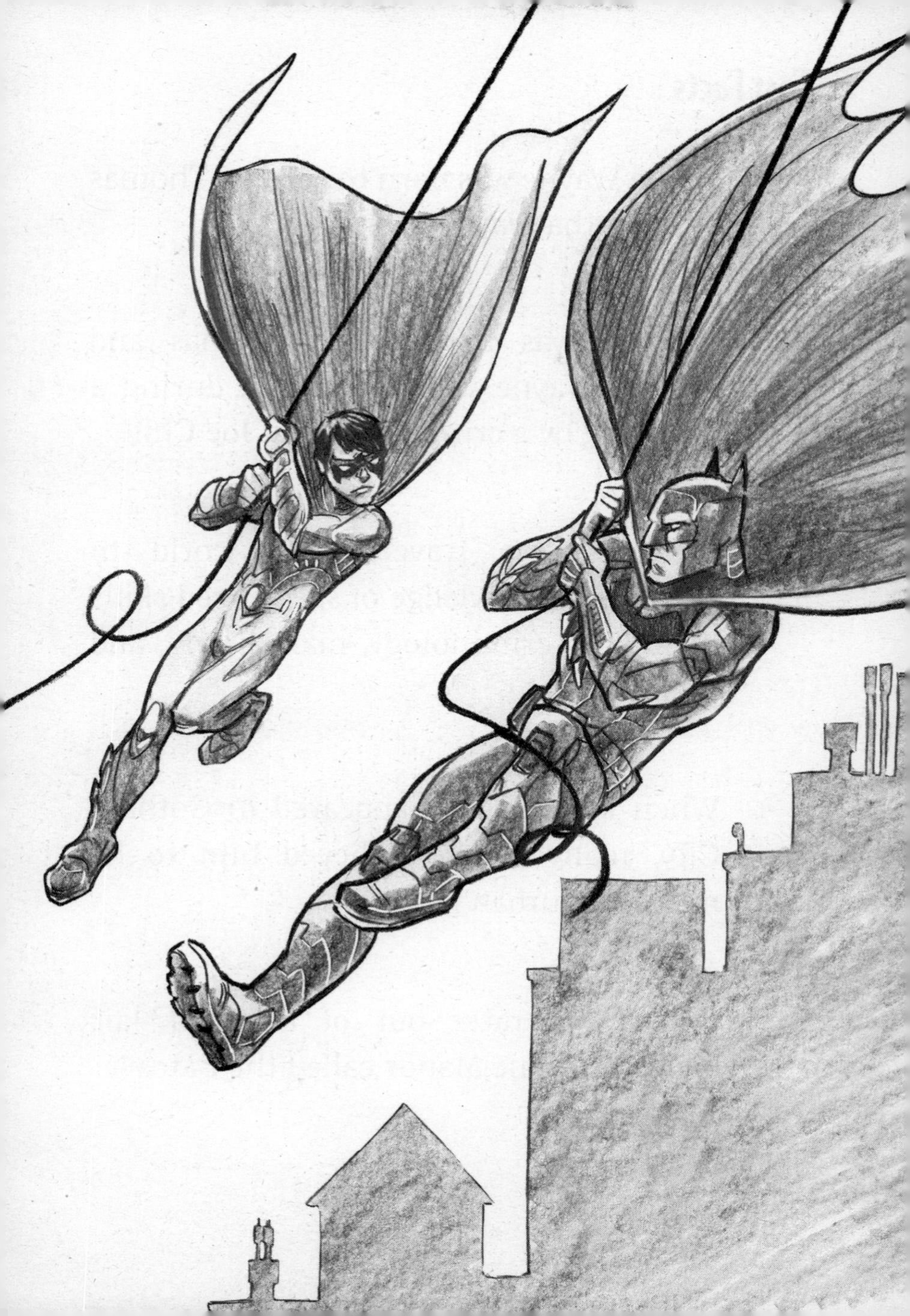

Fast Facts

- Bruce Wayne was born to parents Thomas and Martha Wayne.

- Batman was born when Thomas and Martha Wayne were murdered during a mugging by a criminal named Joe Chill.

- Bruce Wayne traveled the world to perfect his knowledge of specialized skills including: criminology, martial arts, and even acting.

- When Batman first appeared in Gotham City, many people believed him to be merely an urban legend.

- Batman operates out of a secret lair beneath Wayne Manor called the Batcave.

- The Joker used to be a small-time criminal called the Red Hood.

- Batman has partnered with many Robins over the years. These include: Dick Grayson, Jason Todd, Tim Drake, and Bruce Wayne's own son, Damian Wayne.

- The first Robin, Dick Grayson, later took the name Nightwing.

- The daughter of Commissioner James Gordon grew up to become Batgirl.

- Arkham Asylum houses some of the most dangerous criminals ever to face Batman.

- Wayne Manor and the Batcave are located outside of Gotham City in Bristol County.

- One of Bruce Wayne's childhood friends was named Zatanna Zatara. She grew up to be a Super Hero with magical powers simply called Zatanna.

- As a young boy, Bruce Wayne loved to read detective stories featuring Sherlock Holmes.

- Bruce's father, Thomas Wayne, once dressed as a Batman of sorts during a Halloween party. His costume was part of what inspired Batman to adopt the mantle of the bat.

- Bruce Wayne often used the fake name Frank Dixon when training with experts in order to become the Batman.

- Batman works with the Justice League and Superman. However, he keeps his own emergency supply of Kryptonite in case he ever needs to take down the Man of Steel.

- Batman often pretends to be a criminal named "Matches" Malone in order to learn valuable information from Gotham City's underworld.

- Amadeus Arkham founded Arkham Asylum. He soon grew just as insane as the inmates he housed, and had to be admitted as a patient.

Glossary

allies: A person, organization, state, or country that cooperates or helps another with a particular activity or cause.

cat-o'-nine-tails: A rope whip with nine knotted cords.

chronology: A list of events in order of when they happened.

cowered: Crouching down in fear.

cryogenics: The science that studies the production and effects of very low—very cold—temperatures.

deduce: To discover an idea or fact by reasoning and logic.

despot: A ruler who holds total power, and uses it in cruel or oppressive ways.

eidetic: Able to remember and recall mental images with accurate vividness and detail, as if actually visible.

lair: A secret or private place where someone hides or goes to feel safe or comfortable.

lethal: Harmful or destructive, and able to cause death.

maniacal: Wild, impossible to control, and showing mental madness.

martial arts: Any of the traditional forms of self-defense or combat that utilize physical skill and coordination without weapons.

prolific: Producing or presenting in large numbers.

rogues gallery: A collection of known criminals.

supernatural: From or related to a force beyond scientific understanding or the laws of nature.

swashbuckling: Taking part in daring and romantic adventures while being loud and showing off in an entertaining way.

urban legend: A modern story that no one knows where it came from with little or no supporting facts. It is repeated from person to person and is often humorous or scary.

vigilante: A person or group of people who are not members of law enforcement in their community, but pursue and punish criminals.

ward: A person, usually a minor, under the care and control of a guardian who is not their parent.

A

ACE Chemical Factory, 56
al Ghūl, Rā's, 106–107
al Ghūl, Talia, 77, 80, 106, 108
Aquaman, 83, 85, 86
Arkham, Amadeus, 125
Arkham Asylum, 109, 116, 123, 125

B

Bane, 110, 113
Batarang, 42
Batboat, 43, 48, 50–51
Batcave, 11, 29, 43, 48–49, 122, 123
Batcomputer, 49, 117
Batcycle, 42
Batgirl, 9, 14, 88–93, 123
Bat-Gyro, 43, 46–48
Batman. *See also Wayne, Bruce* (later known as Batman)
  allies, 90–95
  bats, encounter with, 5–6
  beginning of, 5–8, 12–13, 26–28, 30, 55, 71, 122, 124
  costume/Batsuit, 28, 30, 32–34, 36, 93
  equipment, 28, 30, 39–43
  fears, 5–6, 12, 17–19, 102
  foes, 56–69, 96–117
  friends, 23, 67, 69
  Gordon, James, partnership with, 9, 31
  hatred of firearms, 30
  Justice League formed by, 14, 85, 86
  need for a, 119–120
  obsession with, 98, 99
  parents, murder of, 5, 6, 11, 13, 20–21, 23, 122
  Robins working for, 8, 13, 14–15, 70–71, 73–81, 123
  romance, 77, 106, 108
  son, 15, 77, 79–81, 106, 108
  as team player, 84–86, trials to overcome, 55–56, 69
  vehicles, 38–39, 42–48, 50–53
  war on crime, 7, 8, 13, 48
Batmobiles, 38–39, 43–46, 48
Bat-Signal, 31
Batwing, 43, 48, 52–53, 94–95
Birds of Prey, 88–89
Black Canary, 89
Black Mask, 115
Bluebird, 94
Bunker, 87

C

Caped Crusader (Batman nickname), 13, 39, 42, 55, 106, 110
cat o'-nine-tails, 60–61
Catwoman, 10, 60–61, 97
Chill, Joe, 20, 30, 122
circus, 72–73, 110
Clayface, 99, 101

Cobblepot, Oswald (later known as Penguin), 10, 64
cryogenic suit, 103–104
Cyborg, 85–86

D

Dark Knight (Batman nickname), 8, 11, 15, 29, 31
Darkseid, 84
Dent, Harvey, 23, 67–69
Drake, Tim, 14, 77–78, 123
Dynamic Duo, 70, 74

E

eidetic memory, 93
Elliot, Tommy, 115, 117

F

female heroes, *See also Batgirl; Wonder Woman* 89, 124
Firefly, 114–115
Flash, The, 85, 86
Fox, Lucius, 35
Frank Dixon (fake name), 124
freak shows, 110–111

G

global domination, 106
Gordon, Barbara (later known as Batgirl), 9, 91–93
Gordon, James
  background, 31
  daughter, 9, 91, 93, 123
  friends and helpers, 69, 98
Gotham City
  crime in, 6, 55, 93, 97, 114–117, 119–120
  description of, 24
  heroes, 71, 91–95
  keeping safe, 83, 89, 97
  police department, 31, 62, 119
  underworld, 65, 67, 125
grapnel, 40–42
Grayson, Dick (later known as Robin), 8, 13, 15, 71–74, 123
Green Lantern, 85, 86

H

Haly Circus, 72
hang glider, 42–43, 46
heroes, 82–89
Holmes, Sherlock, 124
Hush (Tommy Elliot), 115, 117

I

Iceberg Casino, 66–67

J

Joker
  background and beginning, 9, 13, 56–59, 123
  Catwoman compared to, 61
  challenge presented by, 97
  Harley Quinn's relationship with, 113–114
  second Robin murdered by, 14, 75
Justice League, 14, 84–87, 89, 125

K

Karlo, Basil, 99, 101
Katana, 89
Kid Flash, 87
Killer Croc, 110–111
Killer Moth, 93
Kryptonite, 125
Kyle, Selina (later known as Catwoman), 10, 12, 60–61

L

Langstrom, Dr. Kirk, 104
Lazarus Pits, 75, 106

M

Mad Hatter, 114–115
Man-Bat, 104–106
Mark of Zorro, The (movie), 19
"Matches" Malone (fake name), 125
mental games, 110
Monster Men, 99
Mr. Freeze, 103–104

N

Nightwing (formerly Robin), 8, 15, 74, 123
Nygma, Edward (later known as the Riddler), 11, 61–62, 64

P

Peña Duro, 110
Penguin, the, 10, 13, 64–67
Pennyworth, Alfred, 11, 22, 23, 29, 33
Poison Ivy, 100, 101
Professor Pyg, 115, 117

Q

Quinn, Harley, 59, 113–114
Quinzel, Dr. Harleen, 113–114

R

Ragman, 94
Red Hood (formerly the second Robin), 14, 75
Red Hood (later known as Joker), 9, 13, 56, 58–59, 123
Red Robin (formerly the third Robin), 14, 77, 78, 87
Riddler, the, 11, 12, 61–64, 97
Robin (Damian Wayne), 15, 77, 79–81, 123
Robin (Dick Grayson), 8, 13, 15, 71–75, 123
Robin (Jason Todd), 14–15, 74–77, 123
Robin (Tim Drake), 14, 77, 78, 123
Rogues Gallery, 101, 117

S

Santa Prisca, 110
Scarecrow, 102
Solstice, 87
Strange, Dr. Hugo, 97–99
Superboy, 87
Super Heroes, 84, 86, 124
Superman, 82–83, 85, 86, 125

T

Teen Titans, 87, 89
Thompkins, Leslie, 23, 76
Todd, Jason (later known as Robin), 14–15, 74–77, 123
Two-Face, 68–69

U

Utility Belt, 28, 40–42

V

Ventriloquist, the, 115

W

Wayne, Bruce (later known as Batman)
  as adult, 25, 27–28, 30, 35–37, 71
  background, 8
  bats, encounters with, 5–6, 12, 17–19, 28
  birth, 12, 122
  caves discovered by, 49
  childhood, 12, 13, 16–21, 22–23, 25
  double life, 73
  education and training, 7, 13, 23, 25, 55, 122
  identity, 25, 27–28, 30, 125
  parents, murder of, 5, 6, 11, 13, 16, 20–21, 122
  reading, 124
  son of, 15, 77, 79–81, 123
Wayne, Damian, 15, 77, 79–81, 123
Wayne, Martha, 12, 17, 19, 22, 24
Wayne, Thomas, 12, 17, 19–22, 24, 28, 124
Wayne, Thomas, bust of, 28
Wayne Enterprises, 22, 35
Wayne Foundation, 36
Wayne Manor
  care of, 11
  caverns below, 5, 12, 17, 28, 48–49, 122
  as family home, 22
  fund-raisers at, 36
  grounds, 17
  location, 124
  study, 12, 28
  young residents at, 73
Whirly-Bat, 48
Wonder Girl, 87
Wonder Woman, 82–83, 85, 86
world, saving, 84, 86, 89

Z

Zatanna Zatara (Zatanna), 124
Zorro film, 5, 19